THEN BOWING HIMSELF BACKWARD, TERRAPIN PRECEDED US
INTO THE DINING-ROOM.

THE NOVELS, STORIES AND SKETCHES OF F. HOPKINSON SMITH

THE OTHER FELLOW AND TILE CLUB STORIES ❧ ❧ ❧ ❧ ❧

CHARLES SCRIBNER'S SONS ❧ NEW YORK ❧ 1902

INTRODUCTORY NOTE

LET the boy get down and smell the earth, and let him get down to the level of his kind, helping the weaker man all the time and never forgetting the other fellow.

From *The Man with the Empty Sleeve.*

CONTENTS

vii

CONTENTS

ILLUSTRATIONS

THE OTHER FELLOW

DICK SANDS, CONVICT

I

THE stage stopped at a disheartened-looking tavern with a sagging porch and sprawling wooden steps. A fat man with a good-natured face, tagged with a gray chin whisker, bareheaded, and without a coat, — there was snow on the ground, too, — and who said he was the landlord, lifted my yellow bag from one of the long chintz-covered stage cushions, and preceded me through a sanded hall into a low-ceiled room warmed by a red-hot stove and lighted by windows filled with geraniums in full bloom. The effect of this color was so surprising, and the contrast to the desolate surroundings outside so grateful, that, without stopping to register my name, I drew up a chair and joined the circle of baking loungers. My oversight was promptly noted by the clerk, — a sallow-faced young man with an uncomfortably high collar, red necktie, and stooping shoulders, — and as promptly corrected by his dipping a pen in a wooden inkstand and holding the book on his knee until I could add my own superscription to

3

those on its bespattered page. He had been considerate enough not to ask me to rise.

The landlord studied the signature, his spectacles on his nose, and remarked in a kindly tone, —

"Oh, you 're the man what 's going to lecture to the college."

"Yes ; how far is it from here ?"

" 'Bout two miles out, Bingville way. You 'll want a team, won't you ? If I 'd knowed it was you when yer got out I 'd told the driver to come back for you. But it 's all right — he 's got to stop here again in half an hour — soon 's he leaves the mail."

I thanked him and asked him to see that the stage called for me at half-past seven, as I was to speak at eight o'clock. He nodded in assent, dropped into a rocking chair, and guided a spittoon into range with his foot. Then he backed away a little and began to scrutinize my face. Something about me evidently puzzled him. A leaning mirror that hung over a washstand reflected his head and shoulders, and gave me every expression that flitted across his good-natured countenance.

His summing up was evidently favorable, for his scrutinizing look gave place to a benign smile which widened into curves around his

4

mouth and lost itself in faint ripples under his eyes. Hitching his chair closer, he spread his fat knees, and settled his broad shoulders, lazily stroking his chin whisker all the while with his puffy fingers.

"Guess you ain't been at the business long," he said kindly. " Last one we had, a year ago, looked kinder peaked." The secret of his peculiar interest was now out. "Must be awful tough on yer throat, havin' to holler so. I was n't up to the show, but the fellers said they heard him 'fore they got to the crossin'. 'T was spring weather and the winders was up. He did n't have no baggage — only a paper box and a strap. I got supper for him when he come back, and he did eat hearty — did me good to watch him." Then, looking at the clock and recalling his duties as host, he leaned over, and shielding his mouth with his hand, so as not to be overheard by the loungers, said in a confidential tone, " Supper 'll be on in half an hour, if you want to clean up. I 'll see you get what you want. Your room 's first on the right — you can't miss it."

I expressed my appreciation of his timely suggestion, and picking up the yellow bag myself — hall-boys are scarce in these localities — mounted the steps to my bedroom.

Within the hour, fully equipped in the regulation costume, — swallow-tail, white tie, and
white waistcoat, — I was again hugging the
stove, for my bedroom had been as cold as a
barn.

My appearance created something of a sensa-
tion. A tall man in a butternut suit, with a
sinister face, craned his head as I passed, and
the sallow-faced clerk leaned over the desk in
an absorbed way, his eyes glued to my shirt
front. The others looked stolidly at the red
bulb of the stove. No remarks were made —
none aloud, the splendor of my appearance and
the immaculate nature of my appointments
seeming to have paralyzed general conversation
for the moment. This silence continued. I confess I did not know how to break it. Tavern
stoves are often trying ordeals to the wayfarer ;
the silent listeners with the impassive leather
faces and foxlike eyes disconcert him; he knows
just what they will say about him when they
go out. The awkward stillness was finally
broken by a girl in blue gingham opening a door
and announcing supper.

It was one of those frying-pan feasts of eggs,
bacon, and doughnuts, with canned corn in
birds' bathtubs, plenty of green pickles, and
dabs of home-made preserves in pressed glass

saucers. It occupied a few moments only. When it was over, I resumed my chair by the stove.

The night had evidently grown colder. The landlord had felt it, for he had put on his coat; so had a man with a dyed mustache and heavy red face, whom I had left tipped back against the wall, and who was now raking out the ashes with a poker. So had the butternut man, who had moved two diameters nearer the centre of comfort. All doubts, however, were dispelled by the arrival of a thickset man with ruddy cheeks, who slammed the door behind him and moved quickly toward the stove, shedding the snow from his high boots as he walked. He nodded to the landlord and spread his stiff fingers to the red glow. A faint wreath of white steam arose from his coonskin overcoat, filling the room with the odor of wet horse blankets and burned leather. The landlord left the desk, where he had been figuring with the clerk, approached my chair, and pointing to the new arrival, said, —

"This is the driver I been expectin' over from Hell's Diggings. He'll take you. This man" — he now pointed to me — "wants to go to the college at 7.30."

The new arrival shifted his whip to the other hand, looked me all over, his keen and pene-

7

trating eye resting for an instant on my white shirt and waistcoat, and answered slowly, still looking at me, but addressing the landlord, —

"He 'll have to get somebody else. I got to take Dick Sands over to Millwood Station ; his mother 's took bad again."

"What, Dick Sands ? " came a voice from the other side of the stove. It was the man in the butternut suit.

"Why, Dick Sands," replied the driver in a positive tone.

"Not *Dick Sands* ? " The voice expressed not only surprise but incredulity.

"Yes, DICK SANDS," shouted the driver in a tone that carried with it his instant intention of breaking anybody's head who doubted the statement.

"Gosh ! That so ? When did he git out ? " cried the butternut man.

"Oh, a month back. He 's been up in Hell's Diggin's ever since." Then finding that no one impugned his veracity, he added in a milder tone, "His old mother 's awful sick up to her sister's back of Millwood. He got word awhile ago."

"Well, this gentleman 's got to speak at the college, and our team won't be back in time." The landlord pronounced the word "gentle-

8

man " with emphasis. The white waistcoat had evidently gotten in its fine work.

"Let Dick walk," broke in the clerk. "He's used to it, and used to runnin', too." This last with a dry laugh, in spite of an angry glance from his employer.

" Well, Dick won't walk," snapped the driver, his voice rising. " He'll ride like a white man, he will, and that's all there is to it. His leg's bad ag'in."

These remarks were not aimed at me nor at the room. They were fired point-blank at the clerk. I kept silent; so did the clerk.

" What time was you goin' to take Dick ? " inquired the landlord in a conciliatory tone.

" 'Bout 7.20 — time to catch the 8.10."

" Well, now, why can't you take this man along ? You can go to the Diggings for Dick, and then " — pointing again at me — " you can drop him at the college and keep on to the station. 'T ain't much out of the way."

The driver scanned me closely and answered coldly,—

" Guess his kind don't want to mix in with Dick," and started for the door.

" I have no objection," I answered meekly, "provided I can reach the lecture hall in time."

The driver halted, hit the spittoon squarely in the middle, and said with deep earnestness and with a slight trace of deference, —

"Guess you don't know it all, stranger. Dick's served time. Been up twice."

"Convict?" My voice evidently betrayed my surprise.

"You've struck it fust time — last trip was for five years."

He stood whip in hand, his fur cap pulled over his ears, his eyes fixed on mine, noting the effect of the shot. Every other eye in the room was similarly occupied.

I had no desire to walk to Bingville in the cold. I felt, too, the necessity of proving myself up to the customary village standard in courage and complacency.

"That don't worry me a bit, my friend. There are a good many of us out of jail that ought to be in, and a good many in that ought to be out." I said this calmly, like a man of wide experience and knowledge of the world, one who had travelled extensively, and whose knowledge of convicts and other shady characters was consequently large and varied. The prehistoric age of this epigram was apparently unnoticed by the driver, for he started forward, grasped my hand, and blurted out in a whole-souled, hearty way, strangely in contrast with his former manner, —

"You ain't so gol-darned stuck up, be ye? Yes, I 'll take ye, and glad to." Then he stooped over and laid his hand on my shoulder, and said in a softened voice, "When ye git 'longside o' Dick you tell him that; it 'll please him," and he stalked out and shut the door behind him.

Another dead silence fell upon the group. Then a citizen on the other side of the stove, by the aid of his elbows, lifted himself perpendicularly, unhooked a coat from a peg, and remarked to himself in a tone that expressed supreme disgust, —

"Please him! In a pig's eye it will," and disappeared into the night.

Only two loungers were now left, — the butternut man with the sinister expression, and the red-faced man with the dyed mustache.

The landlord for the second time dropped into a chair beside me.

"I knowed Dick was out, but I did n't say nothing, so many of these fellers 'round here is down on him. The night his time was up Dick come in here on his way home and asked after his mother. He had n't heard from her for a month, and was nigh worried to death about

her. I told him she was all right, and had him
in to dinner. He 'd fleshed up a bit, and nobody did n't catch on who he was, — bein'
away nigh five years, — and so I passed him
off for a drummer.''

At this the red-faced man who had been tilted
back, his feet on the iron rod encircling the stove,
brought them down with a bang, stretched his
arms above his head, and said with a yawn,
addressing the pots of geraniums on the window sill, '' Them as likes jail-birds can have
jail-birds,'' and lounged out of the room, followed by the citizen in butternut. It was apparent that the supper hour of the group had
arrived. It was equally evident that the hospitality of the fireside did not extend to the table.

'' You heard that fellow, did n't you ? '' said
the landlord, turning to me after a moment's
pause. '' You 'd think to hear him talk there
warn't nobody honest 'round here but him.
That 's Chris Rankin — he keeps a rum mill
up to the Forks and sells tanglefoot and groceries to the miners. By Sunday mornin' he 's got
'bout every cent they 've earned. There ain't
a woman in the settlement would n't be glad
if somebody would break his head. I 'd rather
be Dick Sands than him. Dick never drank a
drop in his life, and won't let nobody else if he

can help it. That 's what that slouch hates him for, and that 's what he hates me for.''

The landlord spoke with some feeling — so much so that I squared my chair and faced him to listen the better. His last remark, too, explained a sign tacked over the desk, reading, "No liquors sold here," and which had struck me as unusual when I entered.

"What was this man's crime ? " I asked. "There seems to be some difference of opinion about him.''

" His crime, neighbor, was because there was a lot of fellers that did n't have no common sense ; that 's what his crime was. I 've known Dick since he was knee-high to a barrel o' taters, and there warn't no better " —

"But he was sent up the second time," I interrupted, glancing at my watch, "so the driver said." I had not the slightest interest in Mr. Richard Sands, his crimes or misfortunes.

"Yes, and they 'd sent him up the third time if Judge Polk had lived. The first time it was a pocketbook and three dollars, and the second time it was a ham. Polk did that. Polk 's dead now. God help him if he 'd been alive when Dick got out the last time. First question he asked me after I told him his mother was all right was whether 't was true Polk was

13

dead. When I told him he was he did n't say nothin' at first — just looked down on the floor, and then he said slow-like, —

" ' If Polk had had any common sense, Uncle Jimmy,' — he always calls me ' Uncle Jimmy,' — 'he 'd saved himself a heap o' worry and me a good deal o' sufferin'. I 'm glad he 's dead.' "

II

The driver arrived on the minute, backed up to the sprawling wooden steps, and kicked open the door of the waiting-room with his foot.

" All right, boss, I got two passengers 'stead o' one, but you won't kick, I know. You git in ; I 'll go for the mail." The promotion and the confidential tone were intended as a compliment.

I slipped into my fur overcoat ; slid my manuscript into the outside pocket, and followed the driver out into the cold night. The only light visible came from a smoky kerosene lamp boxed in at the far end of the stage and protected by a pane of glass labelled in red paint, " Fare, ten cents."

Close to its rays sat a man, and close to the man — so close that I mistook her for an overcoat thrown over his arm — cuddled a little girl, the light of the lamp falling directly on her face.

14

She was about ten years of age, and wore a cheap woollen hood tied close to her face, and a red shawl crossed over her chest and knotted behind her back. Her hair was yellow and wea-ther-burned, as if she had played out of doors all her life ; her eyes were pale blue, and her face freckled. Neither she nor the man made any answer to my salutation.

The child looked up into the man's face and shrugged her shoulders with a slight shiver. The man drew her closer to him, as if to warm her the better, and felt her chapped red hands. In the movement his face came into view. He was, perhaps, thirty years of age — wiry and well built, with an oval face ending in a pointed Vandyke beard ; piercing brown eyes, finely chiselled nose, and a well-modelled mouth over which drooped a blond mustache. He was dressed in a dark blue flannel shirt, with loose sailor collar tied with a red 'kerchief, and a black, stiff-brimmed, army-shaped hat a little drawn down over his eyes. Buttoned over his chest was a heavy waistcoat made of a white and gray deerskin, with the hair on the outside. His trousers, which fitted snugly his slender, shapely legs, were tucked into his boot. He wore no coat, despite the cold.

A typical young westerner, I said to myself,

15

— one of the bone and sinew of the land, accustomed to live anywhere in these mountains, cold-proof, of course, or he 'd wear a coat on a night like this. Taking his little sister home, I suppose. The country will never go to the dogs as long as we have these young fellows to fall back upon. Then my eyes rested with pleasure on the pointed beard, the peculiar curve of the hat-brim, the slender waist corrugating the soft fur of the deerskin waistcoat, and the peculiar set of his trousers and boots, like those of an Austrian on parade. And how picturesque, I thought. What an admirable costume for the ideal cowboy or the romantic mountain ranger who comes in at the nick of time to save the young maiden ; and what a hit the favorite of the footlights would make if he could train his physique down to such wire-drawn, alert panther-like outlines and —

A heavy object struck the boot of the stage and interrupted my meditations. It was the mail-bag. The next instant the driver's head was thrust in the door.

" Dick, this is the man I told you was goin' 'long far as Bingville. He 's got a show up to the college."

I started, hardly believing my ears. Shades of D'Artagnan, Davy Crockett, and Daniel

Boone! Could this lithe, well-knit, brown-eyed young Robin Hood be a convict?

" Are you Dick Sands ?" I faltered out.

" Yes, that 's what they call me when I 'm out of jail. When I 'm in I 'm known as One Hundred and Two."

He spoke calmly, quite as if I had asked him his age, — the voice clear and low, with a certain cadence that surprised me all the more. His answer, too, convinced me that the driver had told him of my time-honored views on solitary confinement, and that it had disposed him to be more or less frank toward me. If he expected, however, any further outburst of sympathy from me he was disappointed. The surprise had been so great, and the impression he had made upon me so favorable, that it would have been impossible for me to remind him even in the remotest way of his former misfortunes.

The child looked at me with her pale eyes, and crept still closer, holding on to the man's arm, steadying herself as the stage bumped over the crossings.

For some minutes I kept still, my topics of conversation especially adapted to convicts being limited. Despite my implied boasting to the driver, I had never, to my knowledge, met one before. Then, again, I had not yet adjusted

17

my mind to the fact that the man before me
had ever worn stripes. So I said aimlessly, —

"Is that your little sister?"

"No, I have n't got any little sister," still
in the same calm voice. "This is Ben Mulford's
girl; she lives next to me, and I am taking her
down for the ride. She 's coming back."

The child's hand stole along the man's knee,
found his fingers and held on. I kept silence
for a while, wondering what I would say next.
I felt that to a certain extent I was this man's
guest, and therefore under obligation to preserve the amenities. I began again.

"The driver tells me your mother 's sick?"

"Yes, she is. She went over to her sister's
last week and got cold. She is n't what she
was — I being away from her so much lately.
I got two terms; last time for five years. Every
little thing now knocks her out."

He raised his head and looked at me calmly,
all over, examining each detail, — my derby
hat, white tie, fur overcoat, along my arms to
my gloves, and slowly down to my shoes.

"I s'pose you never done no time?" He
had no suspicion that I had; he only meant to
be amiable.

"No," I said, with equal simplicity, meeting him on his own ground, quite as if an at-

tack of measles at some earlier age was under discussion, to which he had fallen a victim while I had escaped. As he spoke his fingers tightened over the child's hand. Then he turned and straightened her hood, tucking the loose strands of hair under its edge.

"You seem rather fond of that little girl; is she any relation?" I inquired, forgetting that I had asked almost that same question before.

" No, she isn't any relation — just Ben Mulford's girl." He raised his other hand and pressed the child's head down upon the deerskin waistcoat, close into the fur, with infinite tenderness. The child reached up her small, chapped hand and laid it on his cheek, cuddling closer, a shy, satisfied smile overspreading her face.

My topics were exhausted, and we rode on in silence, he sitting in front of me, his eyes now so completely hidden in the shadow of his broad-brimmed hat that I only knew they were fixed on me when some sudden tilt of the stage threw the light full on his face. I tried offering him a cigar, but he would not smoke, — "had gotten out of the habit of it," he said, " being shut up so long. It didn't taste good to him, so he had given it up."

When the stage reached the crossing near

the college gate and stopped, he asked quietly, —

" You get out here ? " and lifted the child as he spoke so that her soiled shoes would not scrape my coat. In the action I saw that his leg pained him, for he bent it suddenly and put his hand on the kneecap.

" I hope your mother will be better," I said. " Good-night; good-night, little girl."

" Thank you ; good-night," he answered quickly, with a strain of sadness that I had not caught before. The child raised her eyes to mine, but did not speak.

I mounted the hill to the big college building, and stopped under a light to look back, following with my eyes the stage on its way to the station. The child was on her knees, looking at me out of the window and waving her hand, but the man sat by the lamp, his head on his chest.

All through my discourse the picture of that keen-eyed, handsome young fellow, with his pointed beard and picturesque deerskin waistcoat, the little child cuddled down upon his breast, kept coming before me.

When I had finished, and was putting on my

coat in the president's room, — the landlord had sent his team to bring me back, — I asked one of the professors, a dry, crackling, sandy-haired professor, with bulging eyes and watch-crystal spectacles, if he knew of a man by the name of Sands who had lived in Hell's Diggings with his mother, and who had served two terms in State's prison; and I related my experience in the stage, telling him of the impression his face and bearing had made upon me, and of his tenderness to the child beside him.

"No, my dear sir, I never heard of him. Hell's Diggings is a most unsafe and unsavory locality. I would advise you to be very careful in returning. The rogue will probably be lying in wait to rob you of your fee;" and he laughed a little harsh laugh that sounded as if some one had suddenly torn a coarse rag.

"But the child with him," I said; "he seemed to love her."

"That's no argument, my dear sir. If he has been twice in State's prison he probably belongs to that class of degenerates in whom all moral sense is lacking. I have begun making some exhaustive investigations of the data obtainable on this subject, which I have embodied in a report, and which I propose sending to the

21

State Committee on the treatment of criminals, and which '' —

" Do you know any criminals personally ? '' I asked blandly, cutting short, as I could see, an extract from the report. His manner, too, strange to say, rather nettled me.

" Thank God, no, sir, — not one ! Do you ? ''

" I am not quite sure," I answered. " I thought I had, but I may have been mistaken.''

III

When I again mounted the sprawling steps of the disheartened-looking tavern, the landlord was sitting by the stove half asleep and alone. He had prepared a little supper, he said, as he led the way, with a benign smile, into the dining-room, where a lonely bracket lamp, backed by a tin reflector, revealed a table holding a pitcher of milk, a saucer of preserves, and some pieces of leather beef about the size used in repairing shoes.

" Come and sit down by me," I said. " I want to talk to you about this young fellow Sands. Tell me everything you know.''

"Well, you saw him ; clean and pert-lookin', ain't he ? Don't look much like a habitual criminal, as Polk called him, does he ? ''

" No, he certainly does not ; but give me

22

the whole story." I was in a mood either to reserve decision or listen to a recommendation of mercy.

"Want me to tell you about the pocketbook or that ham scrape ? "

"Everything from the beginning," and I reached for the scraps of beef and poured out a glass of milk.

" Well, you saw Chris Rankin, did n't you, — that fellow that talked about jail-birds ? Well, one night about six or seven years ago," — the landlord had now drawn out a chair from the other side of the table and was sitting opposite me, leaning forward, his arms on the cloth, — "maybe six years ago, a jay of a farmer stopped at Rankin's and got himself plumb full o' tanglefoot. When he come to pay he hauled out a wallet and chucked it over to Chris and told him to take it out. The wallet struck the edge of the counter and fell on the floor, and out came a wad o' bills. The only other man besides him and Chris in the barroom was Dick. It was Saturday night, and Dick had come in to git his paper, which was always left to Rankin's. Dick seen he was drunk, and he picked the wallet up and handed it back to the farmer. About an hour after that the farmer come a-runnin' in to Ran-

kin's sober as a deacon, a-hollerin' that he'd
been robbed, and wanted to know where Dick
was. He said that he had had two rolls o' bills ;
one was in an envelope with three dollars in it
that he'd got from the bank, and the other was
the roll he paid Chris with. Dick, he claimed,
was the last man who had handled the wallet,
and he vowed he'd stole the envelope with the
three dollars when he handed it back to him.

"When the trial come off everything went
dead ag'in Dick. The cashier of the bank swore
he had given the farmer the money and envelope, and in three new one-dollar bills of the
bank, mind you, for the farmer had sold some
ducks for his wife and wanted clean money for
her. Chris swore he seen Dick pick it up and
fix the money all straight again for the farmer ;
the farmer's wife swore she had took the money
out of her husband's pocket, and that when she
opened the wallet the envelope was gone, and
the farmer, who was so dumb he could n't
write his name, swore that he had n't stopped
no place between Chris Rankin's and home,
'cept just a minute to fix his traces t'other side
of Big Pond Woods.

"Dick's mother, of course, was nigh crazy,
and she come to me and I went and got Lawyer
White. It come up 'fore Judge Polk. After we

had all swore to Dick's good character — and, mind you, there warn't one of 'em could say a word ag'in him 'cept that he lived in Hell's Diggin's — Lawyer White began his speech, claimin' that Dick had always been square as a brick, and that the money must be found on Dick or somewheres nigh him 'fore they could prove he took it.

" Well, the jury was the kind we always git 'round here, and they done what Polk told 'em to in his charge, — just as they always do, — and Dick was found guilty before them fellers left their seats. The mother give a shriek and fell in a heap on the floor, but Dick never changed a muscle nor said a word. When Polk asked him if he had anything to say, he stood up and turned his back on Polk, and faced the court-room, which was jam full, for everybody knowed him and everybody liked him, — you could n't help it.

" ' You people have knowed me here,' Dick says, ' since I was a boy, and you 've knowed my mother. I ain't never in times back done nothin' I was ashamed of, and I ain't now, and you know it. I tell you, men, I did n't take that money.' Then he faced the jury. ' I don't know,' he said, ' as I blame you. Most of you don't know no better, and those o' you who do

25

are afraid to say it; but you, Judge Polk,'
and he squared himself and pointed his finger
straight at him, ' you claim to be a man of ed-
dication, and so there ain't no excuse for you.
You 've seen me grow up here, and if you had
any common sense you 'd know that a man
like me could n't steal that man's money, and
you 'd know, too, that he was too drunk to
know what had become of it.' Then he stopped
and said in a low voice, and with his teeth
set, looking right into Polk's eyes, ' Now I 'm
ready to take whatever you choose to give me,
but remember one thing, — I 'll settle with you
if I ever come back, for puttin' this misery on
to my mother, and don't you forget it.'

" Polk got a little white about the gills, but
he give Dick a year, and they took him away
to Stoneburg.

" After that the mother ran down and got
poorer and poorer, and folks avoided her, and
she got behind and had to sell her stuff, and a
month before his time was out she got sick and
pretty near died. Dick went straight home, and
never left her day nor night, and just stuck to her
and nursed her like any girl would 'a' done, and
got her well again. Of course folks was divided,
and it got red-hot 'round here. Some believed
him innercent, and some believed him guilty.

Lawyer White and fellers like him stuck to him, but Rankin's gang was down on him; and when he come into Chris's place for his paper same as before, all the bums that hang 'round there got up and left, and Chris told Dick he did n't want him there no more. That kinder broke the boy's heart, though he did n't say nothing, and after that he would go off up in the woods by himself, or he 'd go huntin' ches'nuts or picking flowers, all the children after him. Every child in the settlement loved him, and could n't stay away from him. Queer, ain't it, how folks would trust their chil'ren? All the folks in Hell's Diggin's did, anyhow."

"Yes," I interrupted, "there was one with him to-night in the stage."

"That 's right. He always has one or two boys and girls 'long with him; says nothin' ain't honest, no more, 'cept chil'ren and dogs.

"Well, when his mother got 'round ag'in all right, Dick started in to get something to do. He could n't get nothin' here, so he went acrost the mountains to Castleton and got work in a wagon fact'ry. When it come pay-day and they asked him his name he said out loud, Dick Sands, of Hell's Diggin's. This give him away, and the men would n't work with him, and he had to go. I see him the mornin' he got

27

back. He come in and asked for me, and I went out, and he said, ' Uncle Jimmy, they mean I shan't work 'round here. They won't give me no work, and when I git it they won't let me stay. Now, by God ! ' — and he slammed his fist down on the desk, — ' they 'll support me and my mother without workin',' and he went out.   .

"Next thing I heard Dick had come into Rankin's and picked up a ham and walked off with it. Chris, he allus 'lowed, hurt him worse than any one else around here, and so maybe he determined to begin on him. Chris was standin' at the bar when he picked up the ham, and he grabbed a gun and started for him. Dick waited a-standin' in the road, and just as Chris was a-pullin' the trigger, he jumped at him, plantin' his fist in 'tween Chris's eyes. Then he took his gun and went off with the ham. Chris did n't come to for an hour. Then Dick barricaded himself in his house, put his mother in the cellar, strung a row of cartridges 'round his waist, and told 'em to come on. Well, his mother plead with him not to do murder, and after a day he give himself up and come out.

" At the trial the worst scared man was Polk. Dick had dropped in on him once or twice after he got out, tellin' him how he could n't git no work and askin' him to speak up and set him straight with the folks. They do say that Polk never went out o' night when Dick was home, 'fraid he 'd waylay him — though I knew Polk was givin' himself a good deal of worry for no- thin', for Dick warn't the kind to hit a man on the sly. When Polk see who it was a-comin' into court he called the constable and asked if Dick had been searched, and when he found he had he told Ike Martin, the constable, to stand near the bench in case the prisoner got ugly.

"But Dick never said a word, 'cept to say he took the ham and he never intended to pay for it, and he 'd take it again whenever his mother was hungry.

"So Polk give him five years, sayin' it was his second offence, and that he was a 'habitual criminal.' It was all over in half an hour, and Ike Martin and the sheriff had Dick in a buggy and on the way to Stoneburg. They reached the jail about nine o'clock at night, and drove up to the gate. Well, sir, Ike got out on one side and the sheriff he got out on t'other, so they could get close to him when he got down, and, by gosh ! 'fore they knowed where they was at, Dick give a spring clear over the dash- board, and that 's the last they see of him for two months. One day, after they 'd hunted

29

him high and low and lay 'round his mother's
cabin, and jumped in on her half a dozen times
in the middle of the night, hopin' to get him,
— for Polk had offered a reward of five hundred dollars, dead or alive, — Ike come into
my place all het up and his eyes a-hangin' out,
and he say, ' Gimme your long gun, quick ; we
got Dick Sands.' I says, ' How do you know ? '
and he says, ' Some boys seen smoke comin'
out of a mineral hole half a mile up the mountain above Hell's Diggin's, and Dick 's in there
with a bed and blanket, and we 're goin' to
lay for him to-night and plug him when he
comes out if he don't surrender.' And I says,
' You can't have no gun o' mine to shoot Dick,
and if I knowed where he was I 'd go tell him.'
The room was full when he asked for my gun,
and some o' the boys from Hell's Diggin's heard
him and slid off through the woods, and when
the sheriff and his men got there they see the
smoke still comin' up, and lay in the bushes all
night watchin'. 'Bout an hour after daylight
they crep' up. The fire was out and so was
Dick, and all they found was a chicken half
cooked and a quilt off his mother's bed.

" 'Bout a week after that, one Saturday
night, a feller come runnin' up the street from
the market, sayin' Dick had walked into his

30

place just as he was closin' up, — he had a stall
in the public market under the city hall, where
the court is, — and asked him polite as you
please for a cup of coffee and a piece of bread,
and before he could holler Dick was off again
with the bread under his arm. Well, of course,
nobody did n't believe him, for they knowed
Dick warn't darn fool enough to be loafin'
'round a place within twenty foot of the room
where Polk sentenced him. Some said the feller was crazy, and some said it was a put-up
job to throw Ike and the others off the scent.
But the next night Dick, with his gun handy
in the hollow of his arm, and his hat cocked
over his eye, stepped up to the cook shop in
the corner of the market and helped himself to
a pie and a chunk o' cheese right under their
very eyes, and 'fore they could say 'Scat,' he
was off ag'in and did n't leave no more tracks
than a cat.

"By this time the place was wild. Fellers
was gettin' their guns, and Ike Martin was runnin' here and there organizing posses, and most
every other man you 'd meet had a gun and
was swore in as a deputy to git Dick and some
of the five hundred dollars' reward. They hung
'round the market, and they patrolled the
streets, and they had signs and countersigns,

31

and more tomfoolery than would run a circus. Dick lay low and never let on, and nobody did n't see him for another week, when a farmer comin' in with milk 'bout daylight had the life pretty nigh scared out o' him by Dick stopping him, sayin' he was thirsty, and then liftin' the lid off the tin without so much as 'By your leave,' and takin' his fill of the can. 'Bout a week after that the rope got tangled up in the belfry over the courthouse so they could n't ring for fires, and the janitor went up to fix it, and when he came down his legs was shakin' so he could n't stand. What do you think he 'd found ?'' And the landlord leaned over and broke out in a laugh, striking the table with the flat of his hand until every plate and tumbler rattled.

I made no answer.

" By gosh, there was Dick, sound asleep ! He had a bed and blankets and lots o' provisions, and was just as comfortable as a bug in a rug. He 'd been there ever since he got out of the mineral hole ! Tell you I got to laugh whenever I think of it. Dick laughed 'bout it himself t'other day when he told me what fun he had listenin' to Ike and the deputies plannin' to catch him. There ain't another man around here who 'd been smart enough to pick out the

32

belfry. He was right over the room in the courthouse where they was, ye see, and he could
look down 'tween the cracks and hear every
word they said. Rainy nights he 'd sneak out,
and his mother would come down to the market,
and he 'd see her outside. They never tracked
her, of course, when she come there. He told
me she wanted him to go clean away somewheres, but he would n't leave her.

" When the janitor got his breath he busted
in on Ike and the others sittin' 'round swappin'
lies how they 'd catch Dick, and Ike reached
for his gun and crep' up the ladder with two
deputies behind him, and Ike was so scared and
so 'fraid he 'd lose the money that he fired 'fore
Dick got on his feet. The ball broke his leg,
and they all jumped in and clubbed him over
the head and carried him downstairs for dead in
his blankets, and laid him on a butcher's table
in the market, and all the folks in the market
crowded 'round to look at him, lyin' there with
his head hangin' down over the table like a
stuck calf's, and his clothes all bloody. Then
Ike handcuffed him and started for Stoneburg in
a wagon 'fore Dick come to."

" That 's why he could n't walk to-night," I
asked, " and why the driver took him over in
the stage ?"

" Yes, that was it. He 'll never get over it.
Sometimes he 's all right, and then ag'in it hurts
him terrible, 'specially when the weather's bad.

" All the time he was up to Stoneburg them
last four years — he got a year off for good be-
havior — he kept makin' little things and sellin'
'em to the visitors. Everybody went to his cell
— it was the first place the warders took 'em,
and they all bought things from Dick. He had
a nice word for everybody, kind and comforting-
like. He was the handiest feller you ever see.
When he got out he had twenty-nine dollars.
He give every cent to his mother. Warden told
him when he left he had n't had no better man
in the prison since he had been 'p'inted. And
there ain't no better feller now. It 's a darned
mean shame how Chris Rankin and them fellers
is down on him, knowin', too, how it all turned
out.''

I leaned back in my chair and looked at the
landlord. I was conscious of a slight choking in
my throat which could hardly be traced to the
dryness of the beef. I was conscious, too, of a
peculiar affection of the eyes. Two or three
lamps seemed to be swimming around the room,
and one or more blurred landlords were talking
to me with elbows on tables.

" What do you think yourself about that

money of the farmer's ?'' I asked automatically, though I do not think even now that I had the slightest suspicion of his guilt. "Do you believe he stole the three dollars when he handed the wallet back ?''

"Stole 'em ? Not by a d——sight ! Did n't I tell you ? Thought I had. That galoot of a farmer dropped it in the woods 'longside the road when he got out to fix his traces, and he was too full of Chris Rankin's rum to remember it, and after Dick had been sent up for the second time, — the second time, now, mind ye, — and had been in two years for walking off with Rankin's ham, a lot of schoolchildren huntin' for ches'nuts come upon that same envelope in the ditch with them three new dollars in it, covered up under the leaves, and the weeds a-growin' over it. Ben Mulford's girl found it.''

"What, the child he had with him to-night?''

"Yes, little freckle-faced girl with white eyes. Oh, I tell you, Dick 's awful fond of that kid.''

ACCORDING TO THE LAW

I

THE luncheon was at one o'clock. Not one of your club luncheons, served in a silent, sedate mausoleum on the principal street, where your host in the hall below enters your name in a ledger, and a brass-bebuttoned Yellowplush precedes you upstairs into a desolate room furnished with chairs and a round table decorated with pink *boutonnières* set for six, and where you are plied with Manhattans until the other guests arrive.

Nor yet was it one of your smart petticoat luncheons in a Fifth Avenue mansion, where a Delmonico veteran pressed into service for the occasion waves you upstairs to another recruit, who deposits your coat and hat on a bed, and who later on ushers you into a room ablaze with gaslights, — midday, remember, — where you and the other unfortunates are served with English pheasants cooked in their own feathers, or Kennebec salmon embroidered with beets and appliquéd with green mayonnaise. Not that kind of midday meal at all.

On the contrary, it was served, — no, it was eaten, — revelled in, made merry over, in an ancient house fronting on a sleepy old park filled with live-oaks and magnolias, their trunks streaked with green moss and their branches draped with gray crape : an ancient house with a big white door that stood wide open to welcome you, — it was December, too, — and two verandas on either side, stretched out like welcoming arms, their railings half hidden in clinging roses, the blossoms in your face.

There was an old grandmother, too, — quaint as a miniature, — with fluffy white cap and a white worsted shawl and tea-rose cheeks, and a smile like an opening window, so sunny did it make her face. And how delightfully she welcomed us !

I can hear even now the very tones of her voice, and feel the soft, cool, restful touch of her hand.

And there was an old darky, black as a gum shoe, with tufts of grizzled gray wool glued to his temples, — one of those loyal old house servants of the South who belong to a régime that is past. I watched him from the parlor scuffling with his feet as he limped along the wide hall to announce each new arrival (his master's old madeira had foundered him, they said, years

37

before), and always reaching the drawing-room
door long after the newcomer had been welcomed by shouts of laughter and the open arms
of every one in the room : the newcomer another girl, of course.

And this drawing-room, now I think of it,
was not like any other drawing-room that I
knew. Very few things in it matched. The
carpet was a faded red, and of different shades
of repair. The hangings were of yellow silk.
There were haircloth sofas, and a big fireplace,
and plenty of rocking chairs, and lounges covered with chintz of every pattern, and softened
with cushions of every hue.

At one end hung a large mirror made of
squares of glass laid like tiles in a dull gilt frame
that had held it together for nearly a century,
and on the same wall, too, and all so splotched
and mouldy with age that the girls had to
stoop down to pick out a pane clear enough
to straighten their bonnets by.

And on the side wall there were family portraits, and over the mantel queer Chinese por-
celains and a dingy coat of arms in a dingier
frame, and on every table, in all kinds of dishes,
flat and square and round, there were heaps and
heaps of roses — Devonienses, Hermosas, and
Agrippinas — whose distinguished ancestors,

hardy sons of the soil, came direct from the Mayflower (this shall not happen again), and who consequently never knew the enervating influences of a hothouse. And there were marble busts on pedestals, and a wonderful clock on high legs, and medallions with weeping willows of somebody's hair, besides a miscellaneous collection of large and small bric-à-brac, the heirlooms of five generations.

And yet, with all this mismatching of color, form, and style, — this chronological array of fittings and furnishings, beginning with the mouldy mirror and ending with the modern straw chair, — there was a harmony that satisfied one's every sense.

And so restful, and helpful, and comforting, and companionable was it all, and so accustomed was everything to be walked over, and sat on, and kicked about; so glad to be punched out of shape if it were a cushion which you needed for some special curve in your back or twist of your head ; so delighted to be scratched, or slopped over, or scarred full of holes if it were a table that could hold your books or pastepot or lighted pipe ; so hilariously joyful to be stretched out of shape or sagged into irredeemable bulges if it were a straw chair that could soothe your aching bones or rest a tired muscle !

39

When all the girls and young fellows had arrived, — such pretty girls, with such soft, liquid
voices and captivating dialects, the one their
black mammies had taught them, and such un-
conventional, happy young fellows in all sorts
of costumes from blue flannel to broadcloth,
one in a Prince Albert coat and a straw hat in
his hand, and it near Christmas, — the old
darky grew more and more restless, limping in
and out of the open door, dodging anxiously
into the drawing-room and out again, his head
up like a terrapin's.

Finally he veered across to a seat by the
window, and, shielding his mouth with his
wrinkled, leathery paw, bent over the old
grandmother and poured into her ear a commu-
nication of such vital import that the dear old
lady arose at once and, taking my hand, said
in her low, sweet voice that we would wait no
longer for the Judge, who was detained in court.

After this the aged Terrapin scuffled out
again, reappearing almost immediately before
the door in white gloves inches too long at the
fingers. Then bowing himself backwards, he
preceded us into the dining-room.

And the table was so inviting when we took
our seats around it, — I sitting on the right of
the grandmother, being the only stranger, and

the prettiest of all the girls next to me ! And
the merriment was so contagious, and the sal-
lies of wit so sparkling, and the table itself !
Solid mahogany, this old heirloom ! rich and
dark as a meerschaum, the kind of mahogany
that looked as if all the fine old madeira and
choice port that had been drunk above it had
soaked into its pores. And every fibre of it in
evidence, too, except where the silver coasters
and the huge silver centrepiece filled with roses,
and the plates and the necessary appointments
hid its shining countenance.

And the aged Terrapin evidently appreciated
in full the sanctity of this family altar, and duly
realized the importance of his position as its
high priest. Indeed, there was a gravity, a
dignity and repose about him as he limped
through his ministrations which I had noticed
in him before. If he showed any nervousness
at all it was as he glanced now and then toward
the drawing-room door, through which the
Judge must enter.

And yet he appeared outwardly calm, even
under this strain. For had he not provided
for every emergency ? Were not his Honor's
viands already at that moment on the kitchen
hearth, with special plates over them to keep
them hot against his arrival ?

41

And what a luncheon it was! The relays of fried chicken, baked sweet potatoes, corn bread, and mango pickles, — a most extraordinary production, I maintain, is a mango pickle! — and things baked on top and brown, and other things baked on the bottom and creamy white.

And the fun, too, as each course appeared and disappeared only to be followed by something more extraordinary and seductive. The men continued to talk, and the girls never ceased laughing, and the grandmother's eyes constantly followed the Terrapin, giving him mysterious orders with the slightest raising of an eyelash, and we had already reached the salad — or was it the pink baked ham? — when the fairy in the pink waist next me clapped her hands and cried out, —

" Oh, you dear Judge! We waited an hour for you!" — it doubtless seemed long to her — " What in the world kept you?"

" Could n't help it, little one," came a voice in reply; and a man with silver-white hair, dignified bearing, and a sunny smile on his face edged his way around the table to the grandmother, every hand held out to him as he passed, and, bending low over the dear lady, expressed his regrets at having been detained.

Then with an extended hand to me, and " It

gives me very great pleasure to see you in this part of the South, sir," he sat down in the vacant chair, nodding to everybody graciously as he spread his napkin. A moment later he leaned forward and said in explanation to the grandmother, —

" I waited for the jury to come in. You received my message, of course ? "

" Oh, yes, dear Judge ; and although we missed you, we sat down at once."

" Have you been in court all day ? " I asked as an introductory remark. Of course he had if he had waited for the jury. What an extraordinary collection of idiocies one could make if he jotted down all the stupid things said and heard when conversations were being opened.

" Yes, I am sorry to say, trying one of those cases which are becoming daily more common."

I looked up inquiringly.

" Oh, a negro, of course," and the Judge picked up his fork and moved back the wine-glass.

" And such dreadful things happen, and such dreadful creatures are going about ! " said the grandmother, raising her hand deprecatingly.

" How do you account for it, madam ? " I asked. " It was quite different before the war. I have often heard my father tell of the old days, and how much the masters did for their slaves, and how loyal their servants were. I remember one old servant whom we boys called Daddy Billy, who was really one of the family, quite like your " — and I nodded toward the Terrapin, who at the moment was pouring a thin stream of brown sherry into an equally attenuated glass for the special comfort and sustenance of the last arrival.

" Oh, you mean Mordecai," she interrupted, looking at the Terrapin. " He has always been one of our family. How long do you think he has lived with us? " — and she lowered her voice. " Forty-eight years — long before the war — and we love him dearly. My father gave him to us. No, it is not the old house servants, — it is these new negroes, born since the war, that make all the trouble."

" You are right, madam. They are not like Mordecai," and the Judge held up the thin glass between his eye and the light. " God bless the day when Mordecai was born ! I think this is the Amazon sherry, is it not, my dear madam ? "

" Yes, Mordecai's sherry, as we sometimes call it. It may interest you, sir, to hear about it," and she turned to me again. " This wine that the Judge praises so highly was once the

44

pride of my husband's heart, and when Sherman came through and burned our homes, among the few things that were saved were sixty-two bottles of this old Amazon sherry, named after the ship that brought it over. Mordecai buried them in the woods and never told a single soul for two years after — not even my husband. There are a few bottles left, and I always bring one out when we have distinguished guests," and she bowed her head to the Judge and to me. "Oh, yes, Mordecai has always been one of our family, and so has his wife, who is almost as old as he is. She is in the kitchen now, and cooked this luncheon. If these new negroes would only behave like the old ones we should have no trouble," and a faint sigh escaped her.

The Terrapin, who during the conversation had disappeared in search of another hot course for the Judge, had now reappeared, and so the conversation was carried on in tones too low for his ears.

"And has any effort been made to bring these modern negroes, as you call them, into closer relation with you all, and " —

"It would be useless," interrupted the Judge. "The old negroes were held in check by their cabin life and the influence of the 'great house,'

45

as the planter's home was called. All this has passed away. This new product has no home and wants none. They live like animals, and are ready for any crime. Sometimes I think they care neither for wife, child, nor any family tie. The situation is deplorable, and is getting worse every day. It is only the strong hand of the law that now controls these people." His Honor spoke with some positiveness, I thought, and with some warmth.

"But," I broke in, "if when things became more settled you had begun by treating them as your friends," — I was getting into shoal water, but I blundered on, peering into the fog, — "and if you had not looked upon them as an alien race who" —

Just here the siren with the pink waist who sat next me — bless her sweet face! — blew her conch-shell — she had seen the rocks ahead — and cried out, —

"Now, grandma, please stop talking about the war!" (The dear lady had been silent for five minutes.) "We're tired and sick of it, aren't we, girls? And don't you say another word, Judge. You've got to tell us some stories."

A rattle of glasses from all the young people was the response, and the Judge rose, with his hand on his heart and his eyes upraised like

46

those of a dying saint. He protested gallantly that he had n't said a word, and the grandmother insisted with a laugh that she had merely told me about Mordecai hiding the sherry, while I vowed with much solemnity that I had not once opened my lips since I sat down, and called upon the siren in pink to confirm it. To my great surprise she promptly did, with an arch look of mock reproof in her eye ; whereupon, with an atoning bow to her, I grasped the lever, rang "full speed," and thus steamed out into deep water again.

While all this was going on at our end of the table, a running fire of fun had been kept up at the other end, near the young man in the Prince Albert coat, which soon developed into heavy practice, the Judge with infinite zest joining in the merriment, exploding one story after another, each followed by peals of laughter and each better than the other, his Honor eating his luncheon all the while with great gusto as he handled the battery.

During all this the Terrapin neglected no detail of his duty, but served the fifth course to the ladies and the kept-hot courses to the Judge with equal dexterity, and both at the same time, and all without spilling a drop or clinking a plate.

47

When the ladies had withdrawn and we were seated on the veranda fronting the sleepy old park, each man with a rose in his buttonhole, the gift of the girl who had sat next him (the grandmother had pinned the rose she wore at her throat on the lapel of the Judge's coat), and when the Terrapin had produced a silver tray and was about to fill some little egg-shell cups from a George the Third coffee-pot, the Judge, who was lying back in a straw chair, a picture of perfect repose and of peaceful digestion, turned his head slightly toward me and said,

"I am sorry, sir, but I shall be obliged to leave you in a few minutes. I have to sentence a negro by the name of Sam Crouch. When these ladies can spare you it will give me very great pleasure to have you come into court and see how we administer justice to this much abused and much misunderstood race," and he smiled significantly at me.

"What was his crime, Judge?" asked the young man in the Prince Albert coat, as he held out his cup for Mordecai to fill. "Stealing chickens?" The gayety of the table was evidently still with him and upon him.

"No," replied the Judge gravely, and he looked at me, the faintest gleam of triumph in his eyes, "murder."

48

II

There are contrasts in life, sudden transitions from light to dark, startling as those one experiences in dropping from out the light of a spring morning redolent with perfume into the gloom of a coal mine choked with noxious vapors, — out of a morning, if you will, all joy and gladness and the music of many birds; a morning when the wide, white sky is filled with cloud ships drifting lazily; when the trees wave in the freshening wind, and the lark hanging in midair pours out its soul for very joy of living!

And the horror of that other! The never ending night and silence; the foul air reeking with close, stifling odors; the narrow walls where men move as ghosts with heads alight, their bodies lost in the shadows; the ominous sounds of falling rock thundering through the blackness; and again, when all is still, the slow drop, drop of the ooze, like the tick of a death-watch. It is a prison and a tomb, and to those who breathe the sweet air of heaven, and who love the sunshine, the very house of despair.

I myself experienced one of these contrasts when I exchanged all the love and gladness, all the wit and laughter and charm of the luncheon, for the court-room.

It was on the ground floor, level with the grass of the courtyard, which a sudden storm had just drenched. The approach was through a cold, crypt-like passage running under heavy brick arches. At its end hung a door blocked up with slouching ragged figures, craning their woolly heads for a glimpse inside whenever some official or visitor passed in or out.

I elbowed my way past the constables holding long staffs, and, standing on my toes, looked over a sea of heads — a compact mass wedged together as far down as the rail outside the bench. The air was sickening, loathsome, almost unbreathable. The only light, except the dull gray light of the day, came from a single gas-jet flaring over the Judge's head. Every other part of the court-room was lost in the shadow of the passing storm.

Inside the space where the lawyers sat, the floor was littered with torn papers, and the tables were heaped with bundles of briefs and law books in disorder, many of them opened face down.

Behind me rose the gallery reserved for negroes, a loft having no window nor light, hanging like a huge black shadow without form or outline. All over this huge black shadow were spattered specks of white. As I looked again,

I could see that these were the strained eye-
balls and set teeth of motionless negroes.

The Judge, his hands loosely clasped together, sat leaning forward in his seat, his eyes
fastened on the prisoner. The flare of the gas-
jet fell on his stern, immobile face, and cast clear-
lined shadows that cut his profile sharp as a
cameo.

The negro stood below him, his head on his
chest, his arms hanging straight. On either side,
close within reach of the doomed man, were the
sheriffs, rough-looking men with silver shields
on their breasts. They looked straight at the
Judge, nodding mechanically as each word fell
from his lips. They knew the litany.

The condemned man was evidently under
thirty years of age, of almost pure African blood,
well built, and strong. The forehead was low,
the lips heavy, the jaw firm. The brown-black
face showed no cruelty; the eyes were not cun-
ning. It was only a dull, inert face, like those
of a dozen others about him.

As he turned again, I saw that his hair was
cut short, revealing lighter-colored scars on the
scalp, — records of a not too peaceful life, perhaps. His dress was ragged and dingy, patched
trousers, and shabby shoes, and a worn flannel
shirt open at the throat, the skin darker than

the flannel. On a chair beside him lay a crumpled slouch hat, grimed with dirt, the crown frayed and torn.

As I pressed my way farther into the throng toward the bench, the voice of the Judge rose, filling every part of the room, the words falling slowly, as earth drops upon a coffin, " until you be dead, and may God have mercy on your soul ! "

I looked searchingly into the speaker's face. There was not an expression that I could recall, nor a tone in his voice that I remembered. Surely this could not be the same man I had met at the table but an hour before, with that musical laugh and winning smile. I scrutinized him more closely — the rose was still in his buttonhole.

As the voice ceased, the condemned man lifted his face, and turned his head slowly. For a moment his eyes rested on the Judge ; then they moved to the clerks, sitting silent and motionless ; then behind, at the constables, and then up into the black vault packed with his own people.

A deathlike silence met him everywhere.

One of the officers stepped closer. The condemned man riveted his gaze upon him, and held out his hands helplessly ; the officer leaned forward and adjusted the handcuffs. Then came the sharp click of their teeth, like the snap of a hungry wolf.

The two men, — the criminal judged according to the law, and the sheriff, its executor, — chained by their wrists, wheeled about and faced the crowd. The constables raised their staffs, formed a guard, and forced a way through the crowd, the silent gallery following with their eyes until the door closed upon them.

Then through the gloom there ran the audible shiver of pent-up sighs, low whispers, and the stretching of tired muscles.

When I reached the Judge, he was just entering the door of the anteroom opening into his private quarters. His sunny smile had returned, although the voice had not altogether regained its former ring. He said, —

"I trust you were not too late. I waited a few minutes, hoping you had come, and then when it became so dark, I ordered a light lit, but I could n't find you in the crowd. Come in. Let me present you to the district attorney and to the young lawyer whom I appointed to defend the prisoner. While I was passing sentence, they were discussing the verdict. Were you in time for the sentence ?" he continued.

" No," I answered, after shaking hands with both gentlemen and taking the chair which one

of them offered me, " only the last part. But I
saw the man before they led him away, and I
must say he did n't look much like a criminal.
Tell me something about the murder," and I
turned to the young lawyer, a smooth-faced
young man with long black hair tucked behind
his ears, and a frank, open countenance.

"You 'd better ask the district attorney,"
he answered, with a slight shrug of his shoulders. "He is the only one about here who
seems to know anything about the *murder;*
my client, Crouch, did n't, anyhow. I was
counsel for the defence."

He spoke with some feeling, and I thought
with some irritation, but whether because of
his chagrin at losing the case or because of real
sympathy for the negro, I could not tell.

"You seem to forget the jury," answered
the district attorney in a self-satisfied way;
"they evidently knew something about it."
There was a certain elation in his manner, as
he spoke, that surprised me — quite as if he
had won a bet. That a life had been played
for and lost seemed only to heighten his interest in the game.

"No, I don't forget the jury," retorted the
young man, "and I don't forget some of the
witnesses; nor do I forget what you made them

54

say and how you got some of them tangled up.
That negro is as innocent of that crime as I
am. Don't you think so, Judge?" and he
turned to the table and began gathering up his
papers.

His Honor had settled himself in his chair,
the back tipped against the wall. His old manner had returned, so had the charm of his voice.
He had picked up a reed pipe when he entered
the room, and had filled it with tobacco, which
he had broken in finer grains in the palm of his
hand. He was now puffing away steadily to
keep it alight.

"I have no opinion to offer, gentlemen, one
way or the other. The matter, of course, is
closed as far as I am concerned. I think you
will both agree, however, whatever may be
your personal feelings, that my rulings were
fair. As far as I could see, the witnesses told
a straight story, and upon their evidence the
jury brought in the verdict. I think, too, my
charge was just. There was " — here the Judge
puffed away vigorously — " there was, therefore, nothing left for me to do but " — puff —
— puff — " to sentence him. Hang that pipe !
It won't draw," and the Judge, with one of his
musical laughs, rose from his chair and pulled
a straw from the broom in the corner.

The district attorney looked at the discomfited opposing counsel and laughed. Then he added, as an expression of ill-concealed contempt for his inexperience crept over his face, —

" Don't worry over it, my boy. This is one of your first cases, and I know it comes hard, but you 'll get over it before you 've tried as many of them as I have. The nigger had n't a dollar, and somebody had to defend him. The Judge appointed you, and you 've done your duty well, and lost — that 's all there is to it. But I 'll tell you one thing for your information," — and his voice assumed a serious tone, — " and one which you did not notice in this trial, and which you would have done had you known the ways of these niggers as I do, and it went a long way with me in establishing his guilt. From the time Crouch was arrested, down to this very afternoon when the Judge sentenced him, not one of his people has ever turned up, — no father, mother, wife, nor child, — not one."

" That 's not news to me," interrupted the young man. " I tried to get something from Crouch myself, but he would n't talk."

" Of course he would n't talk, and you know why ; simply because he did n't want to be spotted for some other crime. This nigger

56

Crouch '' — and the district attorney looked my way — '' is a product of the war, and one of the worst it has given us, a shiftless tramp that preys on society.'' His remarks were evidently intended for me, for the Judge was not listening, nor was the young lawyer. '' Most of this class of criminals have no homes, and if they have they lie about them, so afraid are they, if they 're fortunate enough to be discharged, that they 'll be rearrested for a crime committed somewhere else.''

'' Which discharge does n't very often happen around here,'' remarked the young man, with a sneer. '' Not if you can help it.''

'' No, which does n't very often happen around here *if I can help it*. You 're right. That 's what I 'm here for,'' the district attorney retorted, with some irritation. '' And now I 'll tell you another thing. I had a second talk with Crouch only this afternoon after the verdict,'' — and he turned to me, — '' while the Judge was lunching with you, sir, and I begged him, now that it was all over, to send for his people, but he was stubborn as a mule, and swore he had no one who would want to see him. I don't suppose he had ; he 's been an outcast since he was born.''

'' And that 's why you worked so hard to

57

hang him, was it ? " The young man was thoroughly angry. I could see the color mount to his cheeks. I could see, too, that Crouch had no friends, except this young sprig of the law, who seemed as much chagrined over the loss of his case as anything else. And yet, I confess, I did not let my sympathies for the under dog get the better of me. I knew enough of the record of this new race not to recognize that there could be two sides to questions like this.

The district attorney bit his lip at the young man's thrust. Then he answered him slowly, but without any show of anger, —

"You have one thing left, you know. You can ask for a new trial. What do you say, Judge ?"

The Judge made no answer. He evidently had lost all interest in the case, for during the discussion he had been engaged in twisting the end of the straw into the stem of the pipe and peering into the clogged bowl with one eye shut.

"And if the Judge granted it, what good would it do ?" burst out the young man as he rose to his feet. "If Sam Crouch had a soul as white as snow, it would n't help him with these juries around here as long as his skin is the

color it is ! '' and he put on his hat and left the
room.

The Judge looked after him a moment and
then said to me, —

''Our young men, sir, are impetuous and
outspoken, but their hearts are all right. I
have n't a doubt but that Crouch was guilty.
He 's probably been a vagrant all his life.''

III

Some weeks after these occurrences I was on
my way South, and again found myself within
reach of the sleepy old park and the gruesome
court-room.

I was the only passenger in the Pullman. I
had travelled all night in this royal fashion —
a whole car to myself — with the porter, a
quiet, attentive young colored man of perhaps
thirty years of age, duly installed as First Gentleman of the Bedchamber, and I had settled
myself for a morning of seclusion, when my pri-
vacy was broken in upon at a way station by
the entrance of a young man in a shooting jacket
and cap, and high boots splashed with mud.

He carried a folding gun in a leather case, an
overcoat, and a game-bag, and was followed by
two dogs. The porter relieved him of his be-
longings, stowed his gun in the rack, hung his

59

overcoat on the hook, and distributed the rest
of his equipment within reach of his hand. Then
he led the dogs back to the baggage car.

The next moment the young sportsman
glanced over the car, rose from his seat, and
held out his hand.

"Have n't forgotten me, have you ? Met
you at the luncheon, you know — time the
Judge was late waiting for the jury to come in."

To my delight and astonishment it was the
young man in the Prince Albert coat.

He proved, as the train sped on, to be a
most entertaining young fellow, telling me of
his sport and the birds he had shot, and of how
good one dog was and how stupid the other,
and how next week he was going after ducks
down the river, and he described a small club-
house which a dozen of his friends had built,
and where, with true Southern hospitality, he
insisted I should join him.

And then we fell to talking about the luncheon, and what a charming morning we had
spent, and of the pretty girls and the dear
grandmother ; and we laughed again over the
Judge's stories, and he told me another, the
Judge's last, which he had heard his Honor tell
at another luncheon ; and then the porter put
up a table, and spread a cloth, and began open-

ing things with a corkscrew, and filling empty glasses with crushed ice and other things, and altogether we had a most comfortable and fraternal and much to be desired half hour.

Just before he left the train — he had to get out at the junction — some further reference to the Judge brought to my recollection that ghostly afternoon in the court-room. Suddenly the picture of the negro with that look of stolid resignation on his face came before me. I asked him if any appeal had been taken in the case, as suggested by the district attorney.

"Appeal ? In the Crouch case ? Not much. Hung him high as Haman."

"When ?"

"'Bout a week ago. And by the way, a very curious thing happened at the hanging. The first time they strung Crouch up the rope broke and let him down, and they had to send eight miles for another. While they were waiting, the mail arrived. The post-office was right opposite. In the bag was a letter for Crouch, care of the warden, but not directed to the jail. The postmaster brought it over and the warden opened it and read it to the prisoner, asking him who it was from, and the nigger said it was from his mother — that the man she worked for had written it. Of course the warden knew it was from Crouch's girl, for Crouch had always sworn he had no family, so the Judge told me. Then Crouch asked the warden if he 'd answer it for him before he died. The warden said he would, and got a sheet of paper, a pen and ink, and sitting down by Crouch under the gallows asked him what he wanted to say. And now, here comes the funny part. All that negro wanted to say was just this : —

"I 'm enjoying good health, and I hope to see you before long.   SAM CROUCH.

"Then Crouch reached over and took the pen out of the warden's hands, and marked a cross underneath what the warden had written, and when the warden asked him what he did that for, he said he wanted his mother to have something he had touched himself. By that time the new rope came, and they swung him up. Curious, was n't it ? The warden said it was the funniest message he ever knew a dying nigger to send, and he 'd hung a good many of 'em. It struck me as being some secret kind of a password. You never can tell about these coons."

"Did the warden mail it ? "

"Oh, yes, of course he mailed it — warden 's square as a brick. Sent it, of course, care of the man the girl works for. He lives somewhere around here, or Crouch said he did. Awfully glad to see you again — I get out here.''

The porter brought in the dogs, I picked up the gun, and we conducted the young sports-man out of the car and into a buggy waiting for him at the end of the platform.

As I entered the car again and waved my hand to him from the open window, I saw a negro woman dart out from the crowd of loun-gers, as if in eager search of some one. She was a tall, bony, ill-formed woman, wearing the rude garb of a farm hand, — blue cotton gown, brown sunbonnet, and the rough muddy shoes of a man.

The dress was faded almost white in parts, and patched with different colors, but looked fresh and clean. It was held together over her flat bust by big bone buttons. There was nei-ther collar nor belt. The sleeves were rolled up above the elbows, showing her strong, muscu-lar arms, tough as rawhide. The hands were large and bony, with big knuckles, the mark of the hoe in the palms.

In her eagerness to speak to the porter the sunbonnet had slipped off. Black as the face was, it brought to my mind, strange to say, those weather-tanned fishwives of the Normandy coast — those sturdy, patient, earnest women, accustomed to toil and exposure, and to the buffetings of wind and tempest.

When the porter appeared on his way back to the car, she sprang forward, and caught him by the arm.

"Oh, I'm dat sorry! An' he ain't come wid ye?" she cried. "But ye see him, did n't ye?" The voice was singularly sweet and musical. "Ye did? Oh, dat's good."

As she spoke, a little black bare-legged picka-ninny, with one garment, ran out from behind the corner of the station, and clung to the wo-man's skirts, hiding her face in their folds. The woman put her hard black hand on the child's cheek, and drew the little woolly head closer to her side.

"Well, when's he comin'? I come dis mawn-in' jes's ye tol' me. An' ye see him, did ye?" she asked, with a strange quivering pathos in her voice.

"Oh, yes, I see him yisterday."

The porter's answer was barely audible. I noticed, too, that he looked away from her as he spoke.

" An' yer sho' now he ain't come wid ye?" and she looked toward the train as if expecting to find some one.

64

"No, he can't come till nex' Saturday," answered the porter.

"Well, I'm mighty dis'pinted. I been a-waitin' an' a-waitin' till I *mos'* gin out. Ain't nobody helped me like him. You tol' me las' time dat he'd be here to-day," and her voice shook. "You tell him I got his letter, an' dat I think 'bout him night an' day, an' dat I'd rudder see him dan anybody in de worl'. And you tell him — an' doan' ye forgit dis — dat you see his sister Maria's chile — dis is her — hol' up yer haid, honey, an' let him see ye. I thought if he come to-day he'd like to see 'er, 'cause he useter tote her roun' on his back when she warn't big'r 'n a shote. An' ye *see* him, did ye? Well, I'm mighty glad o' dat."

She was bending forward, her great black hand on his wrist, her eyes fixed on his. Then a startled, anxious look crossed her face.

"But he ain't sick, dat he didn't come? Yo' *sho'* now, he ain't sick?"

"Oh, no; never see him lookin' so good."

The porter was evidently anxious about the train, for he kept backing away toward his car.

"Well, den, good-by; but doan' ye forgit. Tell him ye see me, an' dat I'm a-hungerin' for him. You hear, *a-hungerin'* for him, an' dat I can't git 'long no mo' widout him. Doan'

65

ye forgit, now, 'cause I mos' daid a-waitin' for him. Good-by.''

The train rolled on. She was still on the platform, her gaunt figure outlined against the morning sky, her eager eyes strained toward us, the child clutching her skirts.

I confess that I have never yet outgrown my affection for the colored race : an affection at best, perhaps, born of the dim, undefined memories of my childhood and of an old black mammy — my father's slave — who crooned over me all day long, and sang me lullabies at night.

I am aware, too, that I do not always carry this affectionate sympathy locked up in a safe, but generally pinned on the outside of my sleeve ; and so it is not surprising, as the hours wore on, and the porter gradually developed his several capacities for making me comfortable, that a certain confidence was established between us.

Then, again, I have always looked upon a Pullman porter as a superior kind of person — certainly among serving people. He does not often think so himself, nor does he ever present to the average mind any marked signs of genius. He is in appearance and deportment

66

very much like all other uniformed attendants belonging to most of the great corporations, — clean, neatly dressed, polite, watchful, and patient. He is also indiscriminate in his ministrations ; for he will gladly open the window for No. 10, and as cheerfully close it one minute later for No. 6. After travelling with him for half a day, you doubtless conclude that nothing more serious weighs on his mind than the duty of regulating the temperature of his car or looking after its linen. But you are wrong.

All this time he is classifying you. He really located you when you entered the car, summing you up as you sought out your berth number. At his first glance he had divined your station in life by your clothes, your personal refinement by your carpet-bag, and your familiarity with travel by the way you took your seat. The shoes he will black for you in the still small hours of the morning, when he has time to think, will give him any other points he requires.

If they are patched or half soled, no amount of diamond shirt studs or watch chain worn with them will save your respectability. If you should reverse your cuffs before him, or imbibe your stimulants from a black bottle which you carry in your inside pocket instead of a silver flask concealed in your bag, no amount of fees will gain for you his unqualified respect. If none of these delinquencies can be laid to your account, and he is still in doubt, he waits until you open your bag.

Should the first rapid glance betray your cigars packed next to your shoes, or the handle of a toothbrush thrust into the sponge-bag, or some other such violation of his standard, your status is fixed ; he knows you. And he does all this while he is bowing and smiling, bringing you a pillow for your head, opening a transom, or putting up wire screens to save you from draughts and dust, and all without any apparent distinction between you and your fellow passengers.

If you swear at him, he will not answer back, and if you smite him, he will nine times out of ten turn to you the other cheek. He does all this because his skin is black, and yours is white, and because he is the servant and representative of a corporation who will see him righted, and who are accustomed to hear complaints. Above all, he will do so because of the wife and children or mother at home in need of the money he earns, and destined to suffer if he lose his place.

He has had, too, if you did but know it, a life

as interesting, perhaps, as any of your acquaintances. It is quite within the possibilities that he has been once or twice to Spain, Italy, or Egypt, depending on the movements of the master he served; that he can speak a dozen words or more of Spanish or Italian or pigeon English, and oftener than not the best English of our public schools; can make an omelette, sew on a button, or clean a gun, and that in an emergency or accident (I know of two who lost their lives to save their passengers) he can be the most helpful, the most loyal, the most human serving man and friend you can find the world over.

If you are selfishly intent on your own affairs, and look upon his civility and his desire to please you as included in the price of your berth or seat, and decide that any extra service he may render you is cancelled by the miserable twenty-five cents which you give him, you will know none of these accomplishments nor the spirit that rules them.

If, however, you are the kind of man who goes about the world with your heart unbuttoned and your earflaps open, eager to catch and hold any little touch of pathos or flash of humor or note of tragedy, you cannot do better than gain his confidence.

69

I cannot say by what process I accomplished this result with this particular porter and on this particular train. It may have been the newness of my shoes, combined with the proper stowing of my toothbrush and the faultless cut of my pajamas ; or it might have been the fact that he had already divined that I liked his race ; but certain it is that no sooner was the woman out of sight than he came direct to my seat, and, with a quiver in his voice, said, —

"Did you see dat woman I spoke to, suh ?"

"Yes ; you did n't seem to want to talk to her."

"Oh, it warn't dat, suh, but dat woman 'bout breaks my heart. Had n't been for de gemman gettin' off here an' me havin' to get his dogs, I would n't 'a' got out de car at all. I hoped she would n't come to-day. I thought she heared 'bout it. Everybody knows it up an' down de road, an' de papers been full, tho' co'se she can't read. She lives 'bout ten miles from here, an' she walked in dis mawnin'. Comes every Saturday. I only makes dis run on Saturday, an' she knows de day I 'm comin'."

"Some trouble ?" I asked.

"Oh, yes, suh, a heap o' trouble ; mo' trouble dan she kin stan' when she knows it. Beats all why nobody ain't done tol' her. I

been talkin' to her every Saturday now for
a month, tellin' her I see him an' dat he 's
a-comin' down, an' dat he sent her his love, an'
once or twice lately I 'd bring her li'l' things
he sent her. Co'se *he* did n't send 'em, 'cause
he was whar he could n't git to 'em, but she
did n't know no better. He 's de only son now
she 'd got, an' he 's been mighty good to her
an' dat li'l' chile she had wid her. I knowed
him ever since he worked on de railroad. Mos'
all de money he gits he gives to her. If he done
the thing they said he done, I ain't got nothin'
mo' to say, but I don't believe he done it, an'
never will. I thought maybe dey 'd let him
go, an' den he 'd come home, an' she would n't
have to suffer no mo'; dat made me keep on
a-lyin' to her.''

"What 's been the matter ? Has he been arrested ?''

"'Rested ! *Rested !* 'Fo' God, suh, dey done
hung him las' week.''

A light began to break in upon me.

"What was his name ?''

"Same name as his mother's, suh — Sam
Crouch.''

CAPTAIN JOE

WANTED — A submarine engineer, experienced in handling heavy stone under water. Apply, etc.

In answer to this advertisement, a man wearing a rough jacket and looking like a sailor opened my office door.

"I'm Captain Joe Bell, out of a job. Seein' your advertisement, I called up. Where is the work, and what is it?"

I explained briefly. A lighthouse was to be built in the "Race," off Fisher's Island, — the foundation of rough stone protected by granite blocks weighing ten tons each. These blocks were to be laid by a diver, as an enrockment, their edges touching. The current in the Race ran six miles an hour. This increased the difficulties of the work.

While my visitor bent over the plans, tracing each detail with a blunted finger that looked like a worn-out thole-pin, I had time to look him over. He was about fifty years of age,

72

CAPTAIN JOE.

powerfully built, short, and as broad as he was long. The very fit of his clothes indicated his enormous strength. His pea-jacket had long since been pulled out of shape in the effort to accommodate itself to the spread of his shoulders. His trousers were corrugated, and halfway up his ankles, in the perpetual struggle to protect equally seat and knee, — each wrinkle outlining a knotted muscle, twisted up and down a pair of legs short and sturdy as rudderposts. His brown hair protruded from under a close-fitting cloth cap, and curled over a neck seamed and bronzed, showing bumps where almost every other man had hollows ; these short curls were streaked with gray. His face was round, ruddy, and wind-tanned, the chin hidden in a stubby beard, which clung to his lower lip ; the mouth was firm, the teeth a row of corn, the jaws strong and determined. Everything about him indicated reserve force, endurance, capacity, and push.

Two things struck me instantly: a voice which was rich and musical, and an eye which looked through me, — a clear, laughing, kindling, tender eye, that changed every instant, boring like a gimlet as he pored over the plans, or lighting up with a flash in the suggestion of ways and means to carry them out.

As he leaned over the table, I noticed that his wrist was bandaged, the cotton wrappings showing beneath his coat-sleeve, discovering a partly healed scar.

"Burnt?" I asked.

"No, scraped. It don't bother now, but it was pretty bad a month back."

"How?"

"Oh, a-wreckin'. I've been four years with the Off-Shore Wreckin' Company. Left yesterday."

"What for?"

He looked straight at me, and said, slowly emphasizing each word, —

"Me and the president did n't gee. He had n't no fault to find with me; but I did n't like his ways, and I quit."

So transparent was his honesty, self-reliance, and grit that such precautionary measures as references or inquiries never once entered my mind. Before he left my room the terms were agreed upon. The following week he took charge of the force, and the work began.

As the summer passed away, the masses of granite were lowered into position, Captain Joe placing each block himself, the steam-lighter holding to her anchors in the rip of the Race.

When the autumn came, a cottage was rented

on the shore of the nearest harbor, and the captain's family of six moved in. Later I noticed two new faces in the home circle, — a pale, sad woman and a delicate-looking child, both dressed in black. They would sometimes remain a week, and then disappear only to return again. The mother was introduced by the captain as " Jennie, widow of my old mate Jim."

" What happened to him, Captain Joe ?" I asked one evening, when she left the room to take the child to bed. He was sitting near the window, from which could be caught a glimpse in the twilight of the tall masts of the schooners, coal-laden, and the jibs of the smacks at anchor near the village wharves.

" Drownded, sir ; two year ago." And he looked the other way.

" Washed overboard ?" I asked, noticing his husky voice.

" No. Smothered in his divin'-dress, with a dumb fool at the other end of his life-line. We wuz to work on the Scotland, sunk in six fathoms of water off Sandy Hook. The president sent for me to come to the city, and I left Jim alone. That week we wuz workin' in her lower hold, Jim and me, I tendin' and Jim divin', and then I goin' below and he lookin' out after my air hose and line. Me bein' away that day, they

75

put a duffer at the pump. Jim got his hose tangled up in a fluke of the anchor; they misunderstood his signals, and hauled taut when they should have eased away. He made a dash at the hose with his knife, but whether it wuz the brass wire wove in it, or because he wuz beat for breath, we don't know. Anyways he warn't strong enough to cut her through, and when they got him up he wuz done for. That wuz mighty rough on me, bein' with Jim mo' 'n ten years, in and out o' water. So I look out for Jennie and the young one. No, it ain't nothin' strange nor new. While I 've got a roof over me she 's welcome. He 'd done the same for me, and I 've got the best of it, for there 's only two of his 'n, and there 's six o' mine."

As the work on the lighthouse progressed, the force and plant increased. A steam-tug was added, stone-sloops were chartered, and the gradual filling up of the interior of the foundation began.

The owner of one of these sloops was a tall, sunken-cheeked old man named Marrows, who lived near the village on a small stone-encrusted farm. Outside of its scanty crop this vessel and her earnings were his sole resource.

Late one afternoon his sloop returned to the harbor with her shrouds loose, her mast started, and her forefoot chewed into splinters. It seemed that her captain, a retired bony fisherman named Barrett, had miscalculated the tide, which cut like a mill-tail in the Race. She had misstayed and swirled, bow on, atop of the enrockment of the lighthouse. When she struck, Captain Joe was in his diving-dress, his helmet off. In a moment he had loosed his heavy iron shoes, caught up a crowbar, and was bounding over the rugged rocks surrounding the foundation, giving quick, sharp orders to his men, who sprang into a yawl and began paying out a heavy line.

The next instant he was under the sloop's bowsprit, his broad back braced against her chains, his legs rigid as hydraulic jacks. Every time the vessel surged he straightened out, concentrating his enormous strength and assisting the backward movement, so that when she lunged again she came a few inches short of the jagged rocks, the wave having spent its force. There he stood for half an hour, shaking his head free from the great sheets of white foam breaking clear over him, shouting his orders between the sousings of the waves, until the men in the yawl had slung a kedge anchor away out astern of the endangered sloop, and she was windlassed clear of the stone pile and saved.

Marrows was on the little dock, peering through the twilight, when his rescued sloop returned to the village harbor. Captain Joe held the tiller. He began as soon as Marrows's gaunt figure, outlined against the evening sky, caught his eye : —

"I tell you, old man, Captain Barrett ain't fittin' to fool round that rock. He 'll get hurt. I tell you he ain't fittin'."

"I believe you, and I 've told him so. Is she sprung, Captain Joe ? "

" A leetle mite forrard, and her mast a touch to starboard, but nothin' to hurt."

" Will she be any good any more ? " Then, as he came nearer, " Why, you 're soaking wet : the boys say you was clear under her." Then, lowering his voice, " You know, Captain Joe, she is a good deal to me."

The captain laid his great rough hand tenderly on the old man's shoulder.

"I know it, I know it ; that 's why I wuz under her chains." Then, raising his voice, " But Barrett ain't fittin' ; mind I tell you he ain't fittin'."

The next day being stormy, with a gale outside and no work possible, Captain Joe tightened up the shrouds of the disabled sloop himself, reset the mast, lecturing Barrett all the

78

while, and then sent word to Marrows that she was "tight as a keg, better 'n ever, and everythin' aboard, 'ceptin' the bony fisherman, who was out of a job."

The winter closed in with the foundation but partly completed. Before the first December gale broke on the rock the derricks were stripped of their rigging and left to battle with the winter's storms, the tools were stowed in the shanty, and all work suspended until the spring. During the long winter that followed, Captain Joe took to the sea, having transferred his diving-gear to the sloop; and before April three coal-laden schooners were anchored, or stranded, as befitted their condition, on the shoals in front of his dock in the village harbor. It made no difference to him how severe was the gale, or how badly strained the helpless vessel, he was under her bottom almost as soon as a line could reach her. Then a patch of canvas, or half a cargo of empty oil-barrels, buoyed her up until the tug could tighten a line over her bow, and tow her to an anchorage inside the light-house. It seemed in truth that winter as if each luckless craft, in its journey up the Sound, did its level best to keep its rail above water long enough to sink peacefully and restfully upon some bar or shoal within reach of Captain Joe's diving-tackle. There it died contented, feeling sure of a speedy resurrection.

If a wrecked schooner, coal-laden, was an unusual sight along the harbor shore, a wrecker distributing her cargo free to his neighbors was a proceeding unknown to the oldest inhabitant. And yet this always occurred when a fresh wreck grounded on the flats.

"That's all right," he would say; "better take a couple of boat-loads more. Seems to me as if we wuz goin' to have a late spring. No, I don't know the price, 'cause I ain't settled with the underwriters; but then she came up mighty easy for me, and a few tons don't make no difference, nohow."

When the settling day came, and his share as salvage was determined upon, there was of course a heavy shortage. He always laughed heartily.

"Better put that down to me," he would say to the agent. "Some of the folks along here boated off a little. Guess they wuz careless, and did n't know how much they took."

Little indiscretions like this soon endeared him to his neighbors. Before long every one up and down the shore knew him, and everybody sent a cheery word flying after him whenever they caught sight of his active, restless figure moving along the vessel's deck, or busy about his dock and wrecking-gear. Even the gruff doctor would crane his head around the edge of his curtained wagon to call out " Good-morning," although he might be clear out of hailing distance.

So passed the winter.

When the first breath of spring blew over the marsh, the shanty for the men on the rock was rebuilt and the work resumed.

During all these months the captain never once referred to his early life or associations, or gave me the slightest clue to his antecedents. Now and then he would speak of Jim, his dead mate, as being a " cur'us square man," and occasionally he would refer to the president of the Off-Shore Wrecking Company, his former employer, as " that skin." Such information as I did gather about his earlier days was fragmentary and disconnected, and generally came from his men, who idolized him, and who had absolute belief in his judgment and the blindest confidence in his ceaseless care for their personal safety. This care was necessary : the swiftness of the current and sudden changes of wind, bringing in a heavy southeast roll, submerging the rock at wave intervals, while the slippery, slimy surface and the frequent falling of the heavy derricks made the work extremely dangerous. He deserved their confidence, for through his constant watchfulness but one man was hurt on the work during the six years of its construction, and this occurred during the captain's absence.

One morning, when tacking across the Race in a small boat in a stiff breeze, with only the captain and myself for crew, I tried to make him talk of himself and his earlier life, and so said suddenly, —

" Oh, Captain Joe ! I met a friend of yours yesterday who wished me to ask you how you stopped the leak in the Hoboken ferry-boat, and why you left the employ of the Off-Shore Wrecking Company."

He raised his eyes quickly, a smile lighting his weather-beaten face.

" Who was it — the president ? " He always spoke of his former employer in that way.

" Yes, — but of one of the big insurance companies ; not your Wrecking Company."

" No, reck'n not. He ought to keep pretty still about it."

" Tell me about it."

" Oh, there ain't nothin' to tell. She got

foul of a tug, and listed some, and I sorter plugged her up till they hauled her into the slip. Been so long ago I 'most forgot about it."

But not another word could be coaxed out of him, except that he remembered that the water was "blamed cold," and his arm was "pretty well tore up for a month."

That night, in the shanty which was built on the completed part of the work, and which sheltered the working force for the three years of this section of the construction, were gathered a crew of a dozen men, many of whom had served with Captain Joe when Jim was alive. While the captain was asleep in the little wooden bunk boarded off for his especial use, the ceaseless thrash of the sea sounding in our ears, I managed, after much questioning and piecing out of personal reminiscences, to gather these details.

One morning in January, two years before, when the ice in the Hudson River ran unusually heavy, a Hoboken ferry-boat slowly crunched her way through the floating floes, until the thickness of the pack choked her paddles in mid-river. The weather had been bitterly cold for weeks, and the keen northwest wind had blown the great fields of floating ice into a hard pack along the New York shore. It was the early morning trip, and the decks were crowded with laboring men, and the driveways choked with teams ; the women and children standing inside the cabins, a solid mass up to the swinging doors. While she was gathering strength for a further effort, an ocean tug sheered to avoid her, veered a point, and crashed into her side, cutting her below the water-line in a great V-shaped gash. The next instant a shriek went up from a hundred throats. Women, with blanched faces, caught terror-stricken children in their arms, while men, crazed with fear, scaled the rails and upper decks to escape the plunging of the overthrown horses. The disabled boat careened from the shock and fell over on her beam helpless. Into the V-shaped gash the water poured a torrent. It seemed but a question of minutes before she would lunge headlong below the ice.

Within two hundred yards of both boats, and free of the heaviest ice, steamed the wrecking tug Reliance of the Off-Shore Wrecking Company, making her way cautiously up the New Jersey shore to coal at Weehawken. On her deck forward, sighting the heavy cakes, and calling out cautionary orders to the mate in the pilot-house, stood Captain Joe. When the ocean tug reversed her engines after the collision and backed clear of the shattered wheel-house of the ferry-boat, he sprang forward, stooped down, ran his eye along the water-line, noted in a flash every shattered plank, climbed into the pilot-house of his own boat, spun her wheel hard down, and before the astonished pilot could catch his breath, ran the nose of the Reliance along the rail of the ferry-boat and dropped upon the latter's deck like a cat.

If he had fallen from a passing cloud, the effect could not have been more startling. Men crowded about him and caught at his hands. Women sank on their knees, and hugged their children, and a sudden peace and stillness possessed every soul on board. Tearing a life-preserver from the man nearest him and throwing it overboard, he backed the coward ahead of him through the swaying mob, ordering the people to stand clear, and forcing the whole mass to the starboard side. The increased weight gradually righted the stricken boat until she regained a nearly even keel.

With a threat to throw overboard any man who stirred, he dropped into the engine-room, met the engineer halfway up the ladder, compelled him to return, dragged the mattresses from the crew's bunks, stripped off blankets, racks of clothes, overalls, cotton waste, and rags of carpet, cramming them into the great rent left by the tug's cutwater, until the space of each broken plank was replaced, except one. Through and over this space the water still combed, deluging the floors and swashing down between the gratings into the hold below.

"Another mattress, quick! All gone? A blanket, then — carpet — anything — five minutes more and she 'll right herself! Quick, for God's sake!"

It was useless. Everything, even to the oil-rags, had been used.

"Your coat, then! Think of the babies, man! Do you hear them?"

Coats and vests were off in an instant; the engineer on his knees bracing the shattered planking, Captain Joe forcing the garments into the splintered openings.

It was useless. Little by little the water gained, bursting out first below, then on one side, only to be recaulked, and only to rush in again.

Captain Joe stood a moment as if undecided, ran his eye searchingly over the engine-room, saw that for his needs it was empty, then deliberately tore down the top wall of caulking he had so carefully built up, and, before the engineer could protest, had forced his own body into

86

the gap with his arm outside level with the drifting ice.

An hour later the disabled ferry-boat, with every soul on board, was towed into the Hoboken slip.

When they lifted him from the wreck, he was unconscious and barely alive. The water had frozen his blood, and the floating ice had torn the flesh from his protruding arm, from shoulder to wrist. When the color began to creep back to his cheeks, he opened his eyes, and said to the doctor who was winding the bandages, —

" Wuz any of them babies hurt ? "

A month passed before he regained his strength, and another week before the arm had healed so that he could get his coat on. Then he went back to his work on board the Reliance.

In the mean time the Off-Shore Wrecking Company had presented a bill to the ferry company for salvage, claiming that the safety of the ferry-boat was due to one of the employees of the Wrecking Company. Payment had been refused, resulting in legal proceedings, which had already begun. The morning following this action Captain Joe was called into the president's office.

"Captain," said that official, "we're going to have some trouble getting our pay for that ferry job. Here's an affidavit for you to swear to."

The captain took the paper to the window and read it through without a comment, then laid it back on the president's desk, picked up his hat, and moved to the door.

"Did you sign it ? "

"No ; and I ain't a-goin' to."

"Why ? "

"'Cause I ain't so durned mean as you be. Look at this arm. Do you think I'd got into that hell-hole if it had n't 'a' been for them women cryin' and the babies a-hollerin' ? And you want 'em to pay for it. If your head wuz n't white, I'd mash it."

Then he walked straight to the cashier, demanded his week's pay, waited until the money was counted out, slammed the office door behind him, and walked out, cursing like a pirate. The next day he answered my advertisement.

The following year, when the masonry was rapidly nearing the top or coping course, and the five years of labor were bringing forth their fruit, the foundation and the pier being then almost ready for the keeper's house and lan-

tern, — its light has flashed a welcome to many
a storm-driven coaster ever since, — I was sitting one lovely spring morning overlooking the
sea, the rock with its cluster of derricks being
just visible far out on the water-line.

Beside me sat a man famous in the literature
of our country, — one who had embalmed in
song and story the heroic deeds of common
men, which are now, and will be, household
words as long as the language is read. To him
I outlined the story, adding, —

"It is but half a mile to the captain's cottage,
and, being Sunday morning, we shall find him
at home ; let him tell it in his own way."

We took the broad road skirting the shore,
overlooking the harbor with its white yachts
glinting against the blue. High up, revelling in
the warm sunlight, the gray gulls poised and
curved, while across the yellow marshes the
tall tower of the harbor light was pencilled
against the morning sky. Over old fences,
patched with driftwood and broken oars and
festooned with fishermen's nets, stretched the
boughs of apple-trees loaded with blossoms,
and in scattered sheltered spots the buttercups
and dandelions brightened the green grass. A
turn in the road, a swinging gate, a flagged path
leading to the porch of a low cottage, and a big

burly fellow held out both hands. It was Captain Joe. He was in his Sunday best, with
white shirt-sleeves, his face clean-shaven to
the very edge of the tuft on his chin.

With a child on each knee, the younger a
newcomer since the building of the lighthouse,
he talked of the " work," his neighbors, the
" wrack " the winter before, — the one on
Fisher's Island, when the captain was drowned,
— the late spring, the cussed sou'east wind that
kep' a-blowin' till you thought it were n't never
goin' to wollup round to the west'ard again ; in
short, of everything — but himself.

My beating the bush with allusions to sinking
vessels, collisions at sea, suits for salvage, and
the like only flushed up such reminiscences as
fall to the lot of seafaring men the world over
— but nothing more. In despair I put the question straight at him.

" Tell him, Captain Joe, of that morning in
the ice off Hoboken, when you boarded the
ferry-boat."

He would, but he had 'most forgot, been so
long ago. So many of these things a-comin' up
when a man 's bangin' round, it 's hard to keep
track on 'em. Remembered there wuz a mess
of people aboard, mostly women and babies,
and they wuz all a-hollerin' to wunst. He wuz

workin' on the Reliance at the time, — captain
of her. Come to think of it, he found her log
last week in his old sea-chest, when he wuz
lookin' for some rubber cloth to patch his divin'-
suit. If his wife would get the book out, he
guessed it wuz all there. He was always par-
tic'ler about keepin' log aboard ship.

When the old well-thumbed book was found,
he perched his glasses on his nose, and began
turning the leaves with that same old thole-pin
of a finger, stopping at every page to remoisten
it, and adding a running commentary of his own
over the long-forgotten records.

"*January 23.*—Yes! that's when we worked
on the Hurricane. She was sunk off Sandy
Hook, loaded with sugar ; nasty mess that. It
wuz somewhere about that time, for I remember
the water wuz pretty cold, and the ice a-runnin'. Ah! here it is. Knowed I had n't forgot
it. You can read it yourself ; my eyes ain't so
good as they wuz " — pointing to the entry on
the ink-stained page.

It read as follows : —

"*January 30.* — Left Jersey City 7 A. M.
Ice running heavy. Captain Joe stopped leak
in ferry-boat."

JONATHAN

HE was so ugly, — outside, I mean : long and lank, flat-chested, shrunken, round-shouldered, stooping when he walked ; body like a plank, arms and legs like split rails, feet immense, hands like paddles, head set on a neck scrawny as a·picked chicken's, hair badly put on and in patches, some about his head, some around his jaws, some under his chin in a half moon, — a good deal on the back of his hands and on his chest. Nature had hewn him in the rough, and had left him with every axe mark showing.

He wore big shoes tied with deer-hide strings, and nondescript breeches that wrinkled along his knotted legs like old gun covers. These were patched and repatched with various hues and textures, — parts of another pair, — bits of a coat and fragments of tailor's cuttings. Sewed in their seat was half of a cobbler's apron, — for greater safety in sliding over ledges and logs, he would tell you. Next came a leather belt polished with use, and then a woollen shirt, —

any kind of a shirt, — cross-barred or striped,
— whatever the store had cheapest, and over
that a waistcoat with a cotton back and some
kind of a front, looking like a state map, it had
so many colored patches. There was never any
coat, — none that I remember. When he wore
a coat he was another kind of a Jonathan, — a
store-dealing Jonathan, or a church-going Jonathan, or a town-meeting Jonathan, — not the
"go-a-fishin'," or "bee-huntin'," or "deer-
stalkin'" Jonathan whom I knew.

There was a wide straw hat, too, that crowned
his head, and canted with the wind, and flopped
about his neck, and would have sailed away
down many a mountain brook but for a faithful
leather strap that lay buried in the half-moon
whiskers and held on for dear life. And from
under the rim of this thatch, and half hidden in
the matted masses of badly adjusted hair, was
a thin, peaked nose, bridged by a pair of big
spectacles, and somewhere below these, again,
a pitfall of a mouth covered with twigs of hair
and an underbrush of beard, while deep set in
the whole tangle, like still pools reflecting the
blue and white of the sweet heavens above,
lay his eyes, — eyes that won you, kindly,
twinkling, merry, trustful, and trusting eyes.
Beneath these pools of light, way down below,

93

way down where his heart beat warm, lived Jonathan.

I know a fruit in Mexico, delicious in flavor, called Timburici, covered by a skin as rough and hairy as a cocoanut; and a flower that bristles with thorns before it blooms into waxen beauty; and there are agates encrusted with clay and pearls that lie hidden in oysters. All these things, somehow, remind me of Jonathan.

His cabin was the last bit of shingle and brick chimney on that side of the Franconia Notch. There were others, farther on in the forest, with bark slants for shelter and forked sticks for swinging kettles; but civilization ended with Jonathan's store-stove and the square of oil-cloth that covered his sitting-room floor. Upstairs, under the rafters, there was a guest chamber smelling of pine boards and drying herbs, and sheltering a bed gridironed with bed-cord and softened by a thin layer of feathers encased in a ticking and covered with a cotton quilt. This bed always made a deep impression upon me mentally and bodily. Mentally, because I always slept so soundly in it whenever I visited Jonathan, — even with the rain pattering on the roof and the wind soughing through the big pine-trees; and bodily, because — well, because of the cords. Beside this bed was a chair for my candle, and on the floor a small square plank, laid loosely over the stovepipe hole which in winter held the pipe.

In summer mornings, Jonathan made an alarm clock of this plank, flopping it about with the end of a fishing-rod poked up from below, never stopping until he saw my sleepy face peering down into his own. There was no bureau, only a nail or so in the scantling, and no washstand, of course ; the tin basin at the well outside was better.

Then there was an old wife that lived in the cabin, — an old wife made of sole leather, with yellow-white hair and a thin, pinched face and a body all angles, — chest, arms, everywhere, — outlined through her straight up and down calico dress. When she spoke, however, you stopped to listen, — it was like a wood sound, low and far away, — soft as a bird call. People living alone in the forests often have these voices.

Last there was a dog, — a mean, snivelling, stump-tailed dog, of no particular breed or kidney. One of those dogs whose ancestry went to the bad many generations before he was born. A dog part fox, — he got all his slyness here ; and part wolf, this made him ravenous ; and part bull-terrier, this made him ill-tempered ;

95

and all the rest poodle, that made him too lazy to move.

The wife knew this dog, and hung the bacon on a high nail out of his reach, and covered with a big dish the pies cooling on the bench ; and the neighbors down the road knew him, and chased him out of their dairy-cellars when he nosed into the milk-pans and cheese-pots ; and even the little children found out what a coward he was, and sent him howling home to his hole under the porch, where he grumbled and pouted all day like a spoiled child that had been half whipped. Everybody knew him, and everybody despised him for a low-down, thieving, lazy cur, — everybody except Jonathan. Jonathan loved him, — loved his weepy, smeary eyes, and his rough black hair, and his fat round body, short stumpy legs, and shorter stumpy tail, — especially the tail. Everything else that the dog lacked could be traced back to the peccadillos of his ancestors, — Jonathan was responsible for the tail.

" Ketched in a b'ar-trap I hed sot up back in thet green timber on Loon Pond Maountin' six year ago last fall, when he wuz a pup," he would say, holding the dog in his lap, — his favorite seat. " I swan, ef it warn't too bad ! Thinks I, when I sot it, I 'll tell the leetle cuss whar it wuz; then — I must hev forgot it. It warn't a week afore he wuz runnin' a rabbet and run right into it. Wall, sir, them iron jaws took thet tail er his'n off julluk a knife. He's allus been kinder sore ag'in me sence, and I dunno but he's right, fur it wuz mighty keerless in me. Wall, sir, he come yowlin' hum, and when he see me he did look saour, — no use talkin', — jest ez ef he wuz a-sayin', ' Yer think you 're paowerful cunnin' with yer b'ar-traps, don't ye ? Jest see what it 's done to my tail. It 's kinder sp'ilt me for a dog.' All my fault, warn't it, George ? " patting his head. (Only Jonathan would call a dog George.)

Here the dog would look up out of one eye as he spoke, — he had n't forgotten the bear-trap, and never intended to let Jonathan forget it either. Then Jonathan would admire ruefully the end of the stump, stroking the dog all the while with his big, hairy, paddle-like hands, George rooting his head under the flap of the parti-colored waistcoat.

One night, I remember, we had waited sup-per, — the wife and I, — we were obliged to wait, the trout being in Jonathan's creel, — when Jonathan walked in, looking tired and worried.

" Hez George come home, Marthy ? " he

asked, resting his long bamboo rod against the porch rail and handing the creel of trout to the wife. "No? Wall, I'm beat ef thet ain't cur'us. Guess I got ter look him up." And he disappeared hurriedly into the darkening forest, his anxious whistling call growing fainter and fainter as he was lost in its depths.

Marthy was not uneasy, — not about the dog; it was the supper that troubled her. She knew Jonathan's ways, and she knew George. This was a favorite trick of the dog's, — this of losing Jonathan.

The trout were about burnt to a crisp and the corn-bread stone cold when Jonathan came trudging back, George in his arms, — a limp, soggy, half-dead dog, apparently. Marthy said nothing. It was an old story. Half the time Jonathan carried him home.

"Supper's ready," she said quietly, and we went in.

George slid out of Jonathan's arms, smelt about for a soft plank, and fell in a heap on the porch, his chin on his paws, his mean little eyes watching lazily, — speaking to nobody, noticing nobody, sulking all to himself. There he stayed until he caught a whiff of the fragrant, pungent odor of fried trout. Then he cocked one eye and lifted an ear. He must not carry things too far. Next I heard a single thump of his six-inch tail. George was beginning to get pleased ; he always did when there were things to eat.

All this time Jonathan, tired out, sat in his big splint chair at the supper-table. He had been thrashing the brook since daylight, — over his knees sometimes. I could still see the high-water mark on his patched trousers. Another whiff of the frying-pan, and George got up. He dared not poke his nose into Marthy's lap, — there were too many chunks of wood within easy reach of her hand. So he sidled up to Jonathan, rubbing his nose against his big knees, whining hungrily, looking up into his face.

"I tell ye," said Jonathan, smiling at me, patting the dog as he spoke, "this yere George hez got more sense 'n most men. He knows what 's become of them trout we ketched. I guess he 's gittin' over the way I treated him to-day. Ye see, we wuz up the East Branch when he run a fox south. Thinks I, the fox 'll take a whirl back and cross the big runway ; and, sure enough, it warn't long afore I heard George a-comin' back, yippin' along up through Hank Simons's holler. So I whistled to him and steered off up onto the maountin' to take a look at Bog-eddy and try and git a pickerel. When I come daown ag'in, I see George warn't

99

whar I left him, so I hollered and whistled ag'in.
Then, thinks I, you 're mad 'cause I left ye,
an' won't let on ye *kin* hear ; so I come along
hum without him. When I went back awhile
ago a-lookin' for him, would yer believe it, thar
he wuz a-layin' in the road, about forty rod this
side of Hank Simons's sugar maples, flat onto
his stummick an' disgusted an' put out awful.
It wuz about all I could do ter git him hum. I
knowed the minute I come in fust time an' see
he warn't here thet his feelin's wuz hurt 'cause
I left him. I presaume mebbe I oughter hollered
ag'in afore I got so fer off. Then I thought, of
course, he knowed I 'd gone to Bog-eddy. Beats
all, what sense some dogs hez.''

I never knew Jonathan to lose patience with
George but once : that was when the dog tried
to burrow into the hole of a pair of chipmunks
whom Jonathan loved. They lived in a tree
blanketed with moss and lying across the wood
road. George had tried to scrape an acquaint-
tance by crawling in uninvited, nearly scaring
the little fellows to death, and Jonathan had
flattened him into the dry leaves with his big,
paddle-like hands. That was before the bear-
trap had nipped his tail, but George never forgot it.

He was particularly polite to chipmunks after

that. He would lie still by the hour and hear Jonathan talk to them without even a whine of discontent. I watched the old man one morning up beneath the ledges, groping on his hands and knees, filling his pockets with nuts and, when he reached the wood road, emptying them in a pile near the chipmunks' tree, George looking on good-naturedly.

"Guess you leetle cunnin's better hurry up," he said, while he poured out the nuts on the ground, his knees sticking up as he sat, like some huge grasshopper's. "Guess ye ain't got more 'n time to fill yer cubbud, — winter 's a-comin' ! Them leetle birches on Bog-eddy is turnin' yeller, — that 's the fust sign. 'Fore ye knows it snow 'll be flyin'. Then whar 'll ye be, with everything froze tighter 'n Sampson bound the heathen, you cunnin' leetle skitterin' pups ! Then I presaume likely ye 'll come a-drulin' raound an' want me an' George should gin ye suthin to git through th' winter on, — won't they, George ?"

"Beats all," he said to me that night, "how thoughtful some dogs is. Had n't been fer George to-day, I 'd clean forgot them leetle folks. I see him scratchin' raound in the leaves, an' I knowed right away what he wuz thinkin' of."

Often when I was sketching in the dense forest, Jonathan would lie down beside me, the
old flop of a hat under his head, his talk rambling on.

"I don't wonder ye like to paint 'em. Thar
hain't nothin' so human ez trees. Take thet big
hemlock right in front er yer. Hain't he led a
pretty decent life ? See how praoud an' tall he 's
growed, with them arms of his'n straight aout
an' them leetle chillen of his'n spraoutin' up
raound him. I tell ye them hemlocks is pretty
decent people. Now take a look at them two
white birches down by thet big rock. Ain't it
a shame the way them fellers hez been goin'
on sence they wuz leetle saplin's, makin' it
so nothin' could grow raound 'em, — with ther
jackets all ragged an' tore like tramps, an' ther
toes all out of ther shoes whar ther roots is
stickin' clear of the bark, — ain't they a-ketchin'
it in their ole age ? An' then foller on daown
whar thet leetle bunch er silver maples is dan-
cin' in the sunlight, so slender an' cunnin', —
all aout in ther summer dresses, julluk a bevy
er young gals, — ain't they human like ? I tell
ye, trees is the humanest things thet is."

These talks with me made George restless.
He was never happy unless Jonathan had *him*
on his mind.

JONATHAN

But it was a cluster of daisies that first lifted the inner lid of Jonathan's heart for me. I was away up the side of the Notch overlooking the valley, my easel and canvas lashed to a tree, the wind blew so, when Jonathan came toiling up the slope, a precipice in fact, with a tin can strapped to his back, filled with hot corn and some doughnuts, and threw himself beside me, the sweat running down his weather-tanned neck.

" So long ez we know whar you 're settin' at work, it ain't nat'ral to let ye starve, be it ? " throwing himself beside me. George had started ahead of him, and had been picked up and car- ried, as usual.

When Jonathan sat upright, after a breathing spell, his eye fell on a tuft of limp, bruised daisies, flattened to the earth by the heel of his clumsy shoe. There were acres of others in sight.

" Gosh hang ! " he said, catching his breath suddenly, as if something had stung him, and reaching down with his horny, bent fingers; " ef thet ain't too bad." Then to himself in a tone barely audible, — he had entirely forgotten my presence, — "You never had no sense, Jonathan, nohow, stumblin' raound like er bull calf tramplin' everything. Jes' see what

ye 've gone an' done with them big feet er
yourn," bending over the bruised plant and
tenderly adjusting the leaves. "Them daisies
hez got jest ez good a right ter live ez you
hev."

I was almost sure when I began that I had a
story to tell. I had thought of that one about
Luke Pollard, the day Luke broke his leg behind Loon Mountain, and Jonathan carried him
down the gorge on his back, crossing ledges that
would have scared a goat. It was snowing at
the time, they said, and blowing a gale. When
they got halfway down White Face, Jonathan's
foot slipped and he fell into the ravine, breaking
his wrist. Only the drifts saved his life. Luke
caught a sapling and held on. The doctor set
Jonathan's wrist last, and Luke never knew it
had been broken until the next day. It is one
of the stories they tell you around the stove
winter evenings.

"Julluk the night Jonathan carried aout
Luke," they say, listening to the wind howling
over the ledges.

And then I thought of that other story that
Hank Simons told me, — the one about the mill
back of Woodstock caving in from the freshet
and burying the miller's girl. No one dared lift

the timbers until Jonathan crawled in. The child was pinned down between the beams, and the water rose so fast they feared the wreckage would sweep the mill. Jonathan clung to the sills waist-deep in the torrent, crept under the floor timbers, and then bracing his back held the beam until he dragged her clear. It happened a good many years ago, but Hank always claimed it had bent Jonathan's back.

But, after all, they are not the things I love best to remember of Jonathan.

It is always the old man's voice, crooning his tuneless song as he trudges home in the twilight, his well-filled creel at his side, — the good for nothing dog in his arms ; or it is that look of sweet contentment on his face, — the deep and thoughtful eyes, filled with the calm serenity of his soul. And then the ease and freedom of his life ! Plenty of air and space, and plenty of time to breathe and move ! Having nothing, possessing all things ! No bonds to guard, — no cares to stifle, — no trains to catch, — no appointments to keep, — no fashions to follow, — no follies to shun ! Only the old wife and worthless, lazy dog, and the rod and the creel ! Only the blessed sunshine and fresh, sweet air, and the cool touch of deep woods.

No, there is no story — only Jonathan.

THE MAN WITH THE EMPTY SLEEVE

I

THE Doctor closed the book with an angry gesture and handed it to me as I lay in my steamer chair, my eyes on the tumbling sea. He had read every line in it. So had P. Wooverman Shaw Todd, Esquire, whose property it was, and who had announced himself only a moment before as heartily in sympathy with the pessimistic views of the author, especially in those chapters which described domestic life in America.

The Doctor, who has a wrist of steel and a set of fingers steady enough to adjust a chronometer, and who, though calm and silent as a stone god when over an operating-table, is often as restless and outspoken as a boy when something away from it touches his heartstrings, turned to me and said, —

"There ought to be a law passed to keep these men out of the United States. Here's a Frenchman, now, who speaks no language but his own, and after spending a week at Newport, another at New York, two days at Niagara, and then rushing through the West on a 'Limited,' goes home to give his Impressions of America. Read that chapter on Manners,"and he stretched a hand over my shoulder, turning the leaves quickly with his fingers. "You would think, to listen to these fellows, that all there is to a man is the cut of his coat or the way he takes his soup. Not a line about his being clean and square and alive and all a man, — just manners ! Why, it is enough to make a cast-iron dog bite a blind man."

It would be a waste of time to criticise the Doctor for these irrelevant verbal explosives. Indefensible as they are, they are as much parts of his individuality as the deftness of his touch and the fearlessness of his methods are parts of his surgical training.

P. Wooverman Shaw Todd, Esquire, looked at the Doctor with a slight lifting of his upper lip and a commiserating droop of the eyelid, — an expression indicating, of course, a consciousness of that superior birth and breeding which prevented the possibility of such outbreaks. It was a manner he sometimes assumed toward the Doctor, although they were good friends. P. Wooverman and the Doctor are fellow townsmen and members of the same set, and members, too, of the same club, — a most exclusive club of one hundred. The Doctor had gained admission, not because of his ancestors, etc. (see Log of the Mayflower), but because he had been the first and only American surgeon who had removed some very desirable portions of a gentleman's interior, had washed and ironed them and scalloped their edges, for all I know, and had then replaced them, without being obliged to sign the patient's death certificate the next day.

P. Wooverman Shaw Todd, Esquire, on the other hand, had gained admission because of — well, Todd's birth and his position (he came of an old Salem family who did something in whale oil, — not fish or groceries, be it understood) ; his faultless attire, correct speech, and knowledge of manners and men ; his ability to spend his summers in England and his winters in Nice ; his extensive acquaintance among distinguished people, — the very most distinguished, I know, for Todd has told me so himself, — and — well, all these must certainly be considered sufficient qualifications to entitle any man to membership in almost any club in the world.

P. Wooverman Shaw Todd, Esquire, I say, elevated his upper lip and drooped his eyelid, remarking with a slight Beacon Street accent : —

"I cawn't agree with you, my dear Doctor," — there were often traces of the manners and the bearing of a member of the Upper House in Todd, especially when he talked to a man like the Doctor, who wore turned-down collars and detached cuffs, and who, to quote the distinguished Bostonian, "threw words about like a coal heaver," — "I cawn't agree with you, I say. It is n't the obzervar that we should criticise ; it is what he finds." P. Wooverman was speaking with his best accent. Somehow, the Doctor's bluntness made him over-accentuate it, — particularly when there were listeners about. "This French critic is a man of distinction and a member of the most excloosive circles in Europe. I have met him myself repeatedly, although I cawn't say I know him. We Americans are too sensitive, my dear Doctor. His book, to me, is the work of a keen obzervar who knows the world, and who sees how woefully lacking we are in some of the common civilities of life," and he smiled faintly at me, as if confident that I shared his opinion of the Doctor's own shortcomings. "This Frenchman does not lay it on a bit too thick. Nothing is so mortifying to me as being obliged to travel with a party of Americans who are making their first tour abroad. And it is quite impossible to avoid them, for they all have money and can go where they please. I remember once coming from Basle to Paris, in a first-class carriage, — it was only larst summer, — with a fellow from Indiana or Michigan, or somewhere out there. He had a wife with him who looked like a cook, and a daughter about ten years old, who was a most objectionable young person. You could hear them talk all over the train. I should n't have minded it so much, but Lord Norton's harf-brother was with me," — and P. Wooverman Shaw Todd glanced, as he spoke, at a thin lady with a smelling-bottle and an air of reserve, who always sat with a maid beside her, to see if she were looking at him, — "and one of the best bred men in England, too, and a man who " —

" Now hold on, Todd," broke in the Doctor, upon whom neither the thin lady nor any other listener had made the slightest impression ; " no glittering generalities with me. Just tell me in so many plain words what this man's vulgarity consisted of."

"Why, his manners, his dress, Doctor, — everything about him," retorted Todd.

" Just as I thought ! All you think about is

manners, only manners!" exploded the Doctor. "Your Westerner, no doubt, was a hard-fisted, weather-tanned farmer, who had worked all his life to get money enough to take his wife and child abroad. The wife had tended the dairy and no doubt milked ten cows, and in their old age they both wanted to see something of the world they had heard about. So off they go. If you had any common sense or anything that brought you in touch with your kind, Todd, and had met that man on his own level, instead of overawing him with your high-daddy airs, he would have told you that both the wife and he were determined that the little girl should have a better start in life than their own, and that this trip was part of her education. Do you know any other working people," — and the Doctor faced him squarely, — "any Dutch, or French, or English, Esquimaux or Hottentots, who take their wives and children ten thousand miles to educate them? If I had my way with the shaping of the higher education of the country, the first thing I would teach a boy would be to learn to work, and with his hands, too. We have raised our heroes from the soil, — not from the easy-chairs of our clubs," — and he looked at Todd with his eyebrows knotted tight. "Let the boy get down and smell the earth, and let him get down to the level of his kind, helping the weaker man all the time and never forgetting the other fellow. When he learns to do this, he will begin to know what it is to be a man, and not a manikin.''

When the Doctor is mounted on any one of his hobbies, — whether it is a new microbe, Wagner, or the rights of the workingman, — he is apt to take the bit in his teeth and clear fences. As he finished speaking, two or three of the occupants of contiguous chairs laid down their books to listen. The thin lady with the smelling-bottle and the maid remarked in an undertone to another exclusive passenger on the other side of her, in diamonds and white ermine cape, — it was raining at the time, — that '' one need not travel in a first-class carriage to find vulgar Americans,'' and she glanced from the Doctor to a group of young girls and young men who were laughing as heartily and as merrily, and perhaps as noisily, as if they were sitting on their own front porches at their Southern homes.

Another passenger — who turned out later to be a college professor — said casually, this time to me, that he thought good and bad manners were to be determined, not by externals, but by what lay underneath ; that neither dress, language, nor habits fixed or marred the standard. "A high-class Turk, now," and he lowered his voice, "would be considered ill bred by some people, because in the seclusion of his own family he helps himself with his fingers from the common dish ; and yet so punctili-ously polite and courteous is he that he never sits down in his father's presence nor lights a cigarette without craving his permission."

After this the talk became general, the group taking sides ; some supporting the outspoken Doctor in his blunt defence of his countrymen, others siding with the immaculately dressed Todd, so correct in his every appointment that he was never known, during the whole voyage, to wear a pair of socks that did not in color and design match his cravat.

The chief steward had given us seats at the end of one of the small tables. The Doctor sat under the porthole, and Todd and I had the chairs on either side of him. The two end seats — those on the aisle — were occupied by a girl of twenty-five, simply clad in a plain black dress with plainer linen collar and cuffs, and a young German. The girl would always arrive late, and would sink into her revolving chair with a lan-guid movement, as if the voyage had told upon her. Often her face was pale and her eyes were heavy and red, as if from want of sleep. The young German — a Baron von Hoffbein, the passenger list said — was one of those self-possessed, good-natured, pink-cheeked young Teutons, with blue eyes, blond hair, and a tiny waxed mustache, a mere circumflex accent of a mustache, over his "o" of a mouth. His sponsors in baptism had doubtless sent him across the sea to chase the wild boar or the rude buffalo, with the ultimate design, perhaps, of founding a brewery in some Western city.

The manners of this young aristocrat toward the girl were an especial source of delight to Todd, who watched his every movement with the keenest interest. Whenever the baron approached the table he would hesitate a moment, as if in doubt as to which particular chair he should occupy, and, with an apologetic hand on his heart and a slight bow, drop into a seat immediately opposite hers. Then he would raise a long, thin arm aloft and snap his fingers to call a passing waiter. I noticed that he always ordered the same breakfast, beginning with cold sausage and ending with pancakes. During the repast the young girl opposite him would talk to him in a simple, straightforward way, quite as a sister would have done, and without the slightest trace of either coquetry or undue reserve.

When we were five days out, a third person occupied a seat at one side of the young woman. He was a man of perhaps sixty years of age, with big shoulders and big body, and a great round head covered with a mass of dull white hair which fell about his neck and forehead. The newcomer was dressed in a suit of gray cloth, much worn and badly cut, the coat collar, by reason of the misfit, being hunched up under his hair. This gave him the appearance of a man without a shirt collar, until a turn of his head revealed his clean starched linen and narrow black cravat. He looked like a plain, well-to-do manufacturer or contractor, one whose earlier years had been spent in the out of doors; for the weather had left its mark on his neck, where one can always look for signs of a man's manner of life. His was that of a man who had worn low-collared flannel shirts most of his days. He had, too, a look of determination, as if he had been accustomed to be obeyed. He was evidently an invalid, for his cheeks were sunken and pale, with the pallor that comes of long confinement.

Apart from these characteristics there was nothing specially remarkable about him except the two cavernous eye-sockets, sunk in his head, the shaggy eyebrows arched above them, and the two eyes which blazed and flashed with the inward fire of black opals. As these rested first on one object and then on another, brightening or paling as he moved his head, I could not but think of the action of some alert searchlight gleaming out of a misty night.

As soon as he took his seat, the young wo-man, whose face for the first time since she had been on board had lost its look of anxiety and fatigue, leaned over him smilingly and began adjusting a napkin about his throat and pinning it to his coat. He smiled in response as she fin-ished — a smile of singular sweetness — and held her hand until she regained her seat. They seemed as happy as children or as two lovers, laughing with each other, he now and then stopping to stroke her hand at some word which I could not hear. When, a moment after, the von Hoffbein took his accustomed seat, in full dress, too, — a red silk lining to his waistcoat, and a red silk handkerchief tucked in above it and worn liver-pad fashion, — the girl said sim-ply, looking toward the man in gray, "My fa-ther, sir;" whereupon the young fellow shot up out of his chair, clicked his heels together, crooked his back, placed two fingers on his right eyebrow, and sat down again. The man in gray looked at him curiously and held out his hand, remarking that he was pleased to meet him.

Todd was also watching the group, for I heard him say to the Doctor : "These high-class Germans seldom forget themselves. The young baron saluted the old duffer with the bib as though he were his superior officer."

"Should n't wonder if he were," replied the Doctor, who had been looking intently over his soup spoon at the man in gray, and who was now summing up the circumflex accent, the red edges of the waistcoat, the liver-pad handker-chief, and the rest of von Hoffbein.

"You don't like him, evidently, my dear Doctor."

"You saw him first, Todd — you can have him. I prefer the old duffer, as you call him," answered the Doctor dryly, and put an end to the talk in that direction.

Soon the hum of voices filled the saloon, ris-ing above the clatter of the dishes and the occasional popping of corks. The baron and the man in gray had entered into conversation almost at once, and could be distinctly heard from where we sat, particularly the older man, who was doubtless unconscious of the carrying power of his voice. Such words as "working classes," "the people," "democracy," "when I was in Germany," etc., intermingling with the high-keyed tones of the baron's broken English, were noticeable above the din ; the young girl listening smilingly, her eyes on those of her father. Then I saw the gray man bend forward, and heard him say with great earnestness, and in a voice that could be heard by the occupants of all the tables near our own, —

" It is a great thing to be an American, sir. I never realized it until I saw how things were managed on the other side. It must take all the ambition out of a man not to be able to do what he wants to do and what he knows he can do better than anybody else, simply because somebody higher than he says he shan't. We have our periods of unrest, and our workers sometimes lose their heads, but we always come out right in the end. There is no place in the world where a man has such opportunities as in my country. All he wants is brains and some little horse sense, — the country will do the rest."

Our end of the table had stopped to listen ; so had the occupants of the tables on either side ; so had Todd, who was patting the Doctor's arm, his face beaming.

"Listen to him, Doctor ! Hear that voice ! How like a travelling American ! There 's one of your ex*traw*d'nary clay-soiled sons of toil out on an educating tour : are n't you proud of him ? Oh, it 's too delicious ! "

For once I agreed with Todd. The peculiar strident tones of the man in gray had jarred upon my nerves. I saw, too, that one lady, with slightly elevated shoulder, had turned her back and was addressing her neighbor.

The Doctor had not taken his eyes from the gray man, and had not lost a word of his talk. As Todd finished speaking, the daughter, with all tenderness and with a pleased glance into her father's eyes, arose, and putting her hand in his helped him to his feet, the baron standing at " attention." As the American started to leave the table, and his big shaggy head and broad shoulders reached their full height, the Doctor leaned forward, craning his head eagerly. Then he turned to Todd, and in his crisp, incisive way said, " Todd, the matter with you is that you never see any further than your nose. You ought to be ashamed of yourself. Look at his empty sleeve ; off at the shoulder, too ! "

II

In the smoking-room that night a new and peculiar variety of passenger made his appearance, and his first one, — to me, — although we were then within two days of Sandy Hook. This individual wore a check suit of the latest London cut, big broad-soled Piccadilly shoes, and smoked a brierwood pipe which he constantly filled from a rubber pouch carried in his waistcoat pocket. When I first noticed him, he was sitting at a table with two Englishmen drinking brandy-and-sodas, — plural, not singular.

The Doctor, Todd, and I were at an adjoining table : the Doctor immersed in a scientific pamphlet, Todd sipping his crême de menthe, and I my coffee. Over in one corner were a group of drummers playing poker. They had not left the spot since we started, except at meal-time and at midnight, when Fritz, the smoking-room steward, had turned them out to air the room. Scattered about were other passengers — some reading, some playing checkers or backgammon, others asleep, among them the pink-cheeked von Hoffbein, who lay sprawled out on one of the leather-covered sofas, his thin legs spread apart like the letter A, as he emitted long-drawn organ tones, with only the nose stop pulled out.

The party of Englishmen, by reason of the unlimited number of brandy-and-sodas which their comrade in the check suit had ordered for them, were more or less noisy, laughing a good deal. They had attracted the attention of the whole room, many of the old-timers wondering how long it would be before the third officer would tap the check suit on the shoulder, and send it and him to bed under charge of a steward. The constant admonitions of his companions seemed to have had no effect upon the gentleman in question, for he suddenly launched out upon such topics as Colonial Policies and Governments and Taxation and Modern Fleets ; addressing his remarks, not to his two friends, but to the room at large.

According to my own experience, the travelling Englishman is a quiet, well-bred, reticent man, brandy-and-soda proof (I have seen him drink a dozen of an evening without a droop of an eyelid) ; and if he has any positive convictions of the superiority of that section of the Anglo-Saxon race to which he belongs, — and he invariably has, — he keeps them to himself, certainly in the public smoking-room of a steamer filled with men of a dozen different nations. The outbreak, as well as the effect of the incentive, was therefore as unexpected as it was unusual.

The check-suit man, however, was not constructed along these lines. The spirit of old Hennessy was in his veins, the stored energy of many sodas pressed against his tongue, and an explosion was inevitable. No portion of these excitants, strange to say, had leaked into his legs, for outwardly he was as steady as an undertaker. He began again, his voice pitched in a high key, —

"Talk of coercing England! Why, we 've got a hundred and forty-one ships of the line, within ten days' sail of New York, that could blow the bloody stuffin' out of every man Jack of 'em. And we don't care a brass farthing what Uncle Sam says about it, either."

His two friends tried to keep him quiet, but he broke out again on Colonization and American Treachery and Conquest of Cuba ; and so, being desirous to read in peace, I nodded to the Doctor and Todd, picked up my book, and drew up a steamer chair on the deck outside, under one of the electric lights.

I had hardly settled myself in my seat when a great shout went up from the smoking-room that sent every one running down the deck, and jammed the portholes and doors of the room with curious faces. Then I heard a voice rise clear above the noise inside : " Not another word, sir; you don't know what you are talking about. We Americans don't rob people we give our lives to free."

I forced my way past the door, and stepped inside. The Englishman was being held down in his chair by his two friends. In his effort to break loose he had wormed himself out of his coat. Beside their table, close enough to put his hand on any one of them, stood the Doctor, a curious set expression on his face. Todd was outside the circle, standing on a sofa to get a better view.

Towering above the Englishman, his eyes burning, his shaggy hair about his face, his whole figure tense with indignation, was the man with the empty sleeve! Close behind him, cool, polite, straight as a gendarme, and with the look in his eye of a cat about to spring, stood the young baron. As I reached the centre of the mêlée, wondering what had been the provocation and who had struck the first blow, I saw the baron lean forward, and heard him say in a low voice to one of the Englishmen, "He is so old as to be his fadder; take me," and he tapped his chest meaningly with his fingers. Evidently he had not fenced at Heidelberg for nothing, if he did have pink cheeks and pipestem legs.

The old man turned and laid his hand on the baron's shoulder. "I thank you, sir, but I 'll attend to this young man." His voice had lost all its rasping quality now. It was low and concentrated, like that of one accustomed to command. "Take your hands off him, gentlemen, if you please. I don't think he has so far lost his senses as to strike a man twice his age and with one arm. Now, sir, you will apologize to me, and to the room, and to your own friends, who must be heartily ashamed of your conduct."

At the bottom of almost every Anglo-Saxon is a bed rock of common sense that you reach through the shifting sands of prejudice with the probe of fair play. The young man in the check suit, who was now on his feet, looked the speaker straight in the eye, and, half drunk as he was, held out his hand. "I'm sorry, sir, I offended you. I was speaking to my friends here, and I did not know any Americans were present."

"Bravo!" yelled the Doctor. "What did I tell you, Todd? That's the kind of stuff! Now, gentlemen, all together, — three cheers for the man with the empty sleeve!"

Everybody broke out with another shout, — all but Todd, who had not made the slightest response to the Doctor's invitation to loosen his legs and his lungs. He did not show the slightest emotion over the fracas, and, moreover,

124

seemed to have become suddenly disgusted with the baron.

Then the Doctor grasped the young German by the hand, and said how glad he was to know him, and how delighted he would be if he would join them and " take something," — all of which the young man accepted with a frank, pleased look on his face.

When the room had resumed its normal condition, all three Englishmen having disappeared, the Doctor, whose enthusiasm over the incident had somehow paved the way for closer acquaintance, introduced me in the same informal way both to the baron and to the hero of the occasion as "a brother American," and we all sat down beside the old man, his face lighting up with a smile as he made room for us. Then, laying his hand on my knee, with the manner of an older man, he said, " I ought not to have given way, perhaps; but the truth is, I 'm not accustomed to hear such things at home. I did not know until I got close to him that he had been drinking, or I might have let it pass. I suppose this kind of talk may always go on in the smoking-room of these steamers. I don't know, for it 's my first trip abroad, and on the way out I was too ill to leave my berth. To-night is the first time I 've been in here.

It was bad for me, I suppose. I 've been ill all " —

He stopped suddenly, caught his breath quickly, and his hand fell from my knee. For a moment he sat leaning forward, breathing heavily.

I sprang up, thinking he was about to faint. The baron started for a glass of water. The old man raised his hand.

" No, don't be alarmed, gentlemen ; it is nothing. I am subject to these attacks ; it will pass off in a moment ; " and he glanced around the room as if to assure himself that no one but ourselves had noticed it.

" The excitement was too much for you," the Doctor said gravely, in an undertone. His trained eye had caught the peculiar pallor of the face. " You must not excite yourself so."

" Yes, I know, — the heart," he said after a pause, speaking with short, indrawn breaths, and straightening himself slowly and painfully until he had regained his old erect position. After a little while he put his hand again on my knee, with an added graciousness in his manner, as if in apology for the shock he had given me. " It 's passing off, — yes, I 'm better now." Then in a more cheerful tone, as if to change the subject, he added, " My steward tells me that we made four hundred and fifty-two miles yesterday. This makes my little girl happy. She's had an anxious summer, and I'm glad this part of it is over. Yes, she's *very* happy to-day."

"You mean on account of your health?" I asked sympathetically; although I remembered afterward that I had not caught his meaning.

"Well, not so much that, for that can never be any better, but on account of our being so near home, — only two days more. I could n't bear to leave her alone on shipboard, but it's all right now. You see, there are only two of us since her mother died." His voice fell, and for the first time I saw a shade of sadness cross his face. The Doctor saw it too, for there was a slight quaver in his voice when he said, as he rose, that his stateroom was No. 13, and he would be happy to be called upon at any time, day or night, whenever he could be of service; then he resumed his former seat under the light, and apparently his pamphlet, although I could see his eyes were constantly fixed on the pallid face.

The baron and I kept our seats, and I ordered three of something from Fritz, as further excuse for tarrying beside the invalid. I wanted to know something more of a man who was willing to fight the universe with one arm in defence of his country's good name, though I was still in the dark as to what had been the provocation. All I could gather from the young baron, in his broken English, was that the Englishman had maligned the motives of our government in helping the Cubans, and that the old man had flamed out, astounding the room with the power of his invective and thorough mastery of the subject, and compelling their admiration by the genuineness of his outburst.

"I see you have lost your arm," I began, hoping to get some further facts regarding himself.

"Yes, some years ago," he answered simply, but with a tone that implied he did not care to discuss either the cause or the incidents connected with its loss.

"An accident?" I asked. The empty sleeve seemed suddenly to have a peculiar fascination for me.

"Yes, partly," and, smiling gravely, he rose from his seat, saying that he must rejoin his daughter, who might be worrying. He bade the occupants of the room good-night, many of whom, including the baron and the Doctor, rose to their feet, — the baron saluting, and following the old man out, as if he had been his superior officer.

With the closing of the smoking-room door, P. Wooverman Shaw Todd, Esquire, roused himself from his chair, walked toward the Doctor, and sat down beside him.

"Well! I must say that I 'm glad that man 's gone!" he burst out. "I have never seen anything more outrageous than this whole performance. This fire-eater ought to travel about with a guardian. Suppose, now, my dear Doctor, that everybody went about with these absurd ideas, — what a place the world would be to live in! This is the worst American I have met yet. And see what an example; even the young baron lost his head, I am sorry to say. I heard the young Englishman's remark. It was, I admit, indiscreet, but no part of it was addressed to this very peculiar person; and it is just like that kind of an American, full of bombast and bluster, to feel offended. Besides, every word the young man said was true. There is a great deal of politics in this Cuban business, — you know it, and I know it. We have no men trained for colonial life, and we never shall have, so long as our better clarss keep aloof from politics. The island will be made a camping-ground for vulgar politicians — no question about it. Think, now, of sending that firebrand among those people. You can see by his very appearance that he has never done anything better than astonish the loungers about a country stove. As for all this fuss about his empty sleeve, no doubt some other fire-eater put a bullet through it in defence of what such kind of people call their honor. It is too farcical for words, my dear Doctor, — too farcical for words," and P. Wooverman Shaw Todd, Esquire, pulled his steamer cap over his eyes, jumped to his feet, and stalked out of the room.

The Doctor looked after Todd until he had disappeared. Then he turned to his pamphlet again. There was evidently no composite, explosive epithet deadly enough within reach at the moment, or there is not the slightest doubt in my mind that he would have demolished Todd with it.

Todd's departure made another vacancy at our table, and a tall man, who had applauded the loudest at the apology of the Englishman, dropped into Todd's empty chair, addressing the Doctor as representing our party.

"I suppose you know who the old man is, don't you?"

"No."

"That's John Stedman, manager of the

Union Iron Works of Parkinton, a manufacturing town in my State. He's one of the best iron men in the country. Fine old fellow, is n't he? He's been ill ever since his wife died, and I don't think he 'll ever get over it. She had been sick for years, and he nursed her day and night. He would n't go to Congress, preferring to stay by her, and it almost broke his heart when she died. Poor old man, — don't look as if he was long for this world. I expected him to mop up the floor with that Englishman, sick as he is ; and he would, if he had n't apologized. I heard, too, what your friend who has just gone out said about Stedman not being the kind of a man to send to Cuba. I tell you, they might look the country over, and they could n't find a better. That's been his strong hold, straightening out troubles of one kind or another. Everybody believes in him, and anybody takes his word. He's done a power of good in our State."

"In what way?" asked the Doctor.

"Oh, in settling strikes, for one thing. You see, he started from the scrap pile, and he knows the laboring man down to a dot, for he carried a dinner-pail himself for ten years of his life. When the men are imposed upon, he stands by 'em, and compels the manufacturers to deal square ; and if they don't, he joins the men and fights it out with the bosses. If the men are wrong, and want what the furnaces can't give 'em, — and there's been a good deal of that lately, — he sails into the gangs, and, if nothing else will do, he gets a gun and joins the sheriffs. He was all through that last strike we had, three years ago, and it would be going on now but for John Stedman.''

"But he seems to be a man of fine education,'' interrupted the Doctor, who was listening attentively.

"Yes, so he is, — learned it all at night schools. When he was a boy he used to fire the kilns, and they say you could always find him with a spelling-book in one hand and a chunk of wood in the other, reading nights by the light of the kiln fires.''

"You say he went to Congress ?'' The Doctor's eyes were now fixed on the speaker.

"No, I said he *wouldn't* go. His wife was taken sick about that time, and when he found she wasn't going to get well, — she had lung trouble, — he told the committee that he would n't accept the nomination ; and of course nomination meant election for him. He told 'em his wife had stuck by him all her life, had washed his flannel shirts for him and cooked

132

his dinner, and that he was going to stick by her now she was down. But I tell you what he did do : he stumped the district for his opponent, because he said he was a better man than his own party put up, — and elected him, too. That was just like John Stedman. The heelers were pretty savage, but that made no difference to him.

" He 's never recovered from his wife's death. That daughter with him is the only child he 's got. She 's been so afraid he 'd die on board and have to be buried at sea that he 's kept his berth just to please her. The doctor at home told him Carlsbad was his only chance, and the daughter begged so, he made the trip. He was so sick when he went out that he took a coffin with him, — it 's in the hold now. I heard him tell his daughter this morning that it was all right now, and he thought he 'd get up. You see, there are only two days more, and the captain promised the daughter not to bury her father at sea when we were that close to land. Stedman smiled when he told me, but that 's just like him ; he 's always been cool as a cucumber."

" How did he lose his arm ?" I inquired. I had been strangely absorbed in what he had told me. " In the war ?"

"No. He served two years, but that's not how he lost his arm. He lost it saving the lives of some of his men. I happened to be up at Parkinton at the time, buying some coke, and I saw him carried out. It was about ten years ago. He had invented a new furnace; 'most all the new wrinkles they've got at the Union Company Stedman made for 'em. When they got ready to draw the charge, — that's when the red-hot iron is about to flow out of the furnace, you know, — the outlet got clogged. That's a bad thing to happen to a furnace; for if a chill should set in, the whole plant would be ruined. Then, again, it might explode and tear everything to pieces. Some of the men jumped into the pit with their crowbars, and began to jab away at the opening in the wrong place, and the metal started with a rush. Stedman hollered to 'em to stop; but they either did n't hear him or would n't mind. Then he jumped in among them, threw them out of the way, grabbed a crowbar, and fought the flow until they all got out safe. But the hot metal had about cooked his arm clear to the elbow before he let go."

The Doctor, with hands deep in his pockets, began pacing the floor. Then he stopped, and, looking down at me, said slowly, pointing off his fingers one after the other to keep count as he talked, —

"Tender and loyal to his wife — thoughtful of his child — facing death like a hero — a soldier and patriot. What is there in the make-up of a gentleman that this man has n't got?

"Come! Let 's go out and find that high-collared, silk-stockinged, sweet-scented Anglo-maniac from Salem! By the Eternal, Todd 's got to apologize!"

JOHN SANDERS, LABORER

HE came from up the railroad near the State line. Sanders was the name on the pay roll, — John Sanders, laborer. There was nothing remarkable about him. He was like a hundred others up and down the track. If you paid him off on Saturday night you would have forgotten him the next week, unless, perhaps, he had spoken to you. He looked fifty years of age, and yet he might have been but thirty. He was stout and strong, his hair and beard cropped short. He wore a rough blue jumper, corduroy trousers, and a red flannel shirt, which showed at his throat and wrists. He wore, too, a leather strap buckled about his waist.

If there was anything that distinguished him it was his mouth and eyes, especially when he smiled. The mouth was clean and fresh, the teeth were snow white and regular, as if only pure things came through them; the eyes were frank and true, and looked straight at you without wavering. If you gave him an order, he said, "Yes, sir," never taking his gaze from yours until every detail was complete. When he asked a question, it was to the point and short.

The first week he shovelled coal on a siding, loading the yard engines. Then Burchard, the station-master, sent him down to the street crossing to flag the trains for the dump carts filling the scows at the long dock.

This crossing right-angled a deep railroad cut half a mile long. On the level above, looking down upon its sloping sides, staggered a row of half-drunken shanties with blear-eyed windows, and ragged roofs patched and broken; some hung over on crutches caught under their floor timbers. Sanders lived in one of these cabins, — the one nearest the edge of the granite retaining-wall flanking the street crossing.

Up the slopes of this railroad cut lay the refuse of the shanties, — bottomless buckets, bits of broken chairs, tomato cans, rusty hoops, fragments of straw matting, and other débris of the open lots. In the summer time a few brave tufts of grass, coaxed into life by the warm sun, clung desperately to an accidental level, and now and then a gay dandelion flamed for a day or two and then disappeared, cut off by some bedouin goat. In the winter there were only patches of blackened snow, fouled by the end-less smoke of passing trains, and seamed with the short-cut footpaths of the yard men.

There were only two in Sanders's shanty, — Sanders and his crippled daughter, a girl of twelve, with a broken back. She barely reached the sill when she stood at the low window to watch her father waving his flag. Bent, hollow-eyed, shrunken ; her red hair cropped short in her neck ; her poor little white fingers clutching the window-frame. "The express is late this morning," or "No. 14 is on time," she would say, her restless, eager blue eyes glancing at the clock ; or "What a lot of ashes they do be haulin' to-day ! " Nothing else was to be seen from her window.

When the whistle blew she took down the dinner-pail, filled it with potatoes and the piece of pork hot from the boiling pot, poured the coffee in the tin cup, put on the cover, and, limping to the edge of the retaining-wall, lowered it over by a string to her father. Sanders looked up and waved his hand, and the girl went back to her post at the window.

When the night came, he would light the kerosene lamp in their one room and read aloud the stories from the Sunday papers, she listening eagerly and asking him questions he could not answer, her eyes filling with tears or her face breaking into smiles. This summed up her life.

Not much in the world, all this, for Sanders ! — not much of rest, or comfort, or happy sun-shine, — not much of song or laughter, the pipe of birds or smell of sweet blossoms, — not much room for gratitude or courage or human kind-ness or charity. Only the ceaseless engine-bell, the grime, the sulphurous hellish smoke, the driving rain, the ice and dust, — only the end-less monotony of ill-smelling, steaming carts, the smoke-stained signal-flag and greasy lantern, — only the tottering shanty with the two beds, the stove, and the few chairs and table, — only the blue-eyed crippled girl who wound her thin arms about his neck.

It was on Sundays in the summer that the dreary monotony ceased. Then Sanders would carry her to the edge of the woods, a mile or more back of the cut. There was a little hollow carpeted with violets, and a pond, where now and then a water-lily escaped the factory boys, and there were big trees and bushes and stretches of grass, ending in open lots squared all over by the sod gatherers.

On these days Sanders would lie on his back and watch the treetops swaying in the sunlight against the sky, and the girl would sit by him

139

and make mounds of fresh mosses and pebbles,
and tie the wild flowers into bunches. Sometimes he would pretend that there were fish
in the pond, and would cut a pole and bend
a pin, tie on a bit of string, and sit for hours
watching the cork, she laughing beside him in
expectation. Sometimes they would both go to
sleep, his arm across her. And so the summer
passed.

One day in the autumn, at twelve o'clock
whistle, a crowd of young ruffians from the
bolt-works near the brewery swept down the
crossing chasing a homeless dog. Sanders stood
in the road with his flag. A passing freight
train stopped the mob. The dog dashed between the wheels, doubling, and then bounding
up the slope of the cut, sprang through the half-
open door of the shanty. When he saw the
girl he stopped short, hesitated, looked anxiously into her face, crouched flat, and pulling
himself along by his paws, laid his head at her
feet. When Sanders came home that night the
dog was asleep in her lap. He was about to
drive him out until he caught the look in her
face, then he stopped, and laid his empty dinner-pail on the shelf.

"I seen him a-comin'," he said; "them
rats from the bolt factory was a-humpin' him,

too ! Guess if the freight had n't a-come along they 'd a-ketched him.''

The dog looked wistfully into Sanders's face scanning him curiously, timidly putting out his paw and dropping it, as if he had been too bold and wanted to make some sort of a dumb apology, like a poor relation who has come to spend the day. He had never had any respectable ancestors, — none to speak of. You could see that in the coarse, shaggy hair, like a door mat; the awkward, ungainly walk, the legs doubling under him; the drooping tail with bare spots down its length, suggesting past indignities. He was not a large dog — only about as high as a chair seat; he had mottled lips, too, and sharp, sawlike teeth. One ear was gone, perhaps in his puppyhood, when some one had tried to make a terrier of him and had stopped when half done. The other ear, however, was active enough for two. It would curl forward in attention like a deer's, or start up like a rabbit's in alarm, or lie back on his head when the girl stroked him to sleep. He was only a kickable, chasable kind of a dog, — a dog made for sounding tin pans tied to his tail and whooping boys behind.

All but his eyes ! These were brown as agates, and as deep and clear. Kindly eyes, that looked and thought and trusted. It was these eyes that first made the girl love him ; they reminded her, strange to say, of her father's. She saw, too, perhaps unconsciously to herself, down in their depths, something of the same hunger for sympathy that stirred her own heart — the longing for companionship. She wanted something nearer her own age to love, though she never told her father. This was a heartache she kept to herself, perhaps because she hardly understood it.

The dog and the girl became inseparable. At night he slept under her bed, reaching his head up in the gray dawn, and licking her face until she covered him up warm beside her. When the trains passed he would stand up on his hind legs, his paws on the sill, his blunt little nose against the pane, whining at the clanging bells, or barking at the great rings of steam and smoke coughed up by the engines below.

She taught him all manner of tricks. How to walk on his hind feet with a paper cap on his head, a plate in his mouth, begging. How to make believe he was dead, lying still a minute at a time, his odd ear furling nervously and his eyes snapping fun. How to carry a basket to the grocery on the corner, when she would limp out in the morning for a penny's worth

142

of milk or a loaf of bread, he waiting until she crossed the street, and then marching on proudly before her.

With the coming of the dog a new and happier light seemed to have brightened the shanty. Sanders himself began to feel the influence. He would play with him by the hour, holding his mouth tight, pushing back his lips so that his teeth glistened, twirling his ear. There was a third person now for him to consult and talk to. "It 'll be turrible cold at the crossin' to-day, won't it, Dog?" or "Thet's No. 23 puffin' up in the cut: don't yer know her bell? Wonder, Dog, what she's switched fur?" he would say to him. He noticed, too, that the girl's cheeks were not so white and pinched. She seemed taller and not so weary; and when he walked up the cut, tired out with the day's work, she always met him at the door, the dog springing halfway down the slope, wagging his tail and bounding ahead to welcome him. And she would sing little snatches of songs that her mother had taught her years ago, before the great flood swept away the cabin and left only her father and herself clinging to a bridge, she with a broken back.

After a while Sanders coaxed him down to the track, teaching him to bring back his empty

143

dinner-pail, the dog spending the hour with him, sitting by his side demurely, or asleep in the sentry-box.

All this time the dog never rose to the dignity of any particular name. The girl spoke of him as "Doggie," and Sanders always as "the Dog." The trainmen called him "Rags," in deference, no doubt, to his torn ear and threadbare tail. They threw coal at him as he passed, until it leaked out that he belonged to "Sanders's girl." Then they became his champions, and this name and pastime seemed out of place. Only once did he earn any distinguishing sobriquet. That was when he had saved the girl's basket, after a sharp fight with a larger and less honest dog. Sanders then spoke of him, with half-concealed pride, as "the Boss," but this only lasted a day or so. Publicly, in the neighborhood, he was known as "Sanders's dog."

One morning the dog came limping up the cut with a broken leg. Some said a horse had kicked him ; some that the factory boys had thrown stones at him. He made no outcry, only came sorrowfully in, his mouth dry and dust-covered, dragging his hind leg, that hung loose like a flail ; then he laid his head in the girl's lap. She crooned and cried over him all day, binding up the bruised limb, washing his

144

eyes and mouth, putting him in her own bed. There was no one to go for her father, and if there were, he could not leave the crossing. When Sanders came home, he felt the leg over carefully, the girl watching eagerly. "No, Kate, child, yees can't do nothin'; it's broke at the jint. Don't cry, young one."

Then he went outside and sat on a bench, looking across the cut and over the roofs of the factories, hazy in the breath of a hundred furnaces, and so across the blue river fringed with waving trees where the blessed sun was sinking to rest. He was not surprised. It was like everything else in his life. When he loved something, it was sure to be this way.

That night, when the girl was asleep, he took the dog up in his arms, and wrapping his coat around him so the corner loafers could not see, rang the bell of the dispensary. The doctor was out, but a nurse looked at the wound. "No, there was nothing to be done; the socket had been crushed. Keep it bandaged, that was all." Then he brought him home and put him under the bed.

In three or four weeks he was about again, dragging the leg when he walked. He could still get around the shanty and over to the grocer's, but he could not climb the hill, even with the pail empty. He tried one day, but he climbed only halfway. Sanders found him in the path when he went home, lying down by the pail.

Sanders worried over the dog. He missed the long talks at the crossing over the dinner, the poor fellow sitting by his side watching every spoonful, his eyes glistening, the old ear furling and unfurling like a toy flag. He missed, too, his scampering after the sparrows and pigeons that often braved the desolation and smoke of this inferno to pick up the droppings from the carts. He missed more than all the companionship, — somebody to sit beside him.

As for the girl, there was now a double bond between her and the dog. He was not only poor and an outcast, but a cripple like herself. Before, she was his friend, now, she was his mother, whispering to him, her cheek to his; holding him up to the window to see the trains rush by, his nose touching the glass, his poor leg dangling.

The train hands missed him too, vowing vengeance, and the fireman of No. 6, Joe Connors, spent half a Sunday trying to find the boy that threw the stone. Bill Adams, who ran the yard engine, went all the way home the next day after the accident for a bottle of horse lini-

ment, and left it at the shanty, and said he 'd
get the doctor at the next station if Sanders
wanted.

One broiling hot August day, — a day when
the grasshoppers sang among the weeds in the
open lot, and the tar dripped down from the
roofs ; when the teams strained up the hill reeking with sweat, a wet sponge over their eyes,
and the drivers walked beside their carts mop-
ping their necks, — on one of these steaming August days the dog limped down to the crossing
just to rub his nose once against Sanders as he
stood waving his flag, or to look wistfully up
into his face as he sat in the little pepper-box
of a house that sheltered his flags and lantern.
He did not often come now. They were making
up the local freight — the yard engine backing
and shunting the cars into line. Bill Adams
was at the throttle and Connors was firing. A
few yards below Sanders's sentry-box stood an
empty flat car on a siding. It threw a grateful
shade over the hard cinder-covered tracks. The
dog had crawled beneath its trucks and lay
asleep, his stiffened leg over the switch frog.
Adams's yard engine puffing by woke him with
a start. There was a struggle, a yell of pain,
and the dog fell over on his back, his useless
leg fast in the frog. Sanders heard the cry of

147

agony, threw down his flag, bounded over the cross-ties, and crawled beneath the trucks. The dog's cries stopped. But the leg was fast. In a moment more he had rushed back to his box, caught up a crowbar, and was forcing the joint. It did not give an inch. There was but one thing left, — to throw the switch before the express, due in two minutes, whirled past. In another instant a man in a blue jumper was seen darting up the tracks. He sprang at a lever, bounded back, and threw himself under the flat car. Then the yelp of a dog in pain, drowned by the shriek of an engine dashing into the cut at full speed. Then a dog thrown clear of the track, a crash like a falling house, and a flat car smashed into kindling wood.

When the conductor and passengers of the express walked back, Bill Adams was bending over a man in a blue jumper laid flat on the cinders. He was bleeding from a wound in his head. Lying beside him was a yellow dog licking his stiffened hand. A doctor among the passengers opened his red shirt and pressed his hand on the heart. He said he was breathing, and might live. Then they brought a stretcher from the office, and Connors and Bill Adams carried him up the hill, the dog following, limping.

JOHN SANDERS, LABORER

Here they laid him on a bed beside a sobbing, frightened girl ; the dog at her feet.

Adams bent over him, washing his head with a wad of cotton waste.

Just before he died he opened his eyes, rested them on his daughter, half raised his head as if in search of the dog, and then fell back on his bed, that same sweet, clear smile about his mouth.

"John Sanders," said Adams, "how in h—— could a sensible man like you throw his life away for a damned yellow dog ? "

"Don't, Billy," he said. "I could n't help it. He was a cripple."

HUTCHINS

HUTCHINS lived at the foot of the hill, in a battered, patched-up shanty of broken windows and half-hinged doors. The neighbors told queer stories about this rookery, and when they could, passed by on the other side. Time had stained its unpainted boards a dull gray. Untidy women hung about the porch crowded with washtubs, while cooking utensils, broken pots, and fragments of a rusty summer stove littered the steps and outhouse roof.

The only spot that defied the filth and squalor was a little patch of a garden shut in by a broken fence. This held a dozen rows of corn, a stray stalk of morning-glory clinging to a bent and tottering pole, a flaming stand of hollyhock, and a few overgrown sprouts of turnip rioting in the freedom of their neglect.

Hutchins himself, except at rare intervals, always leaned lazily in the propped-up doorway, a ragged, dirt-begrimed tramp, biting savagely at the end of a clay pipe. Besotted, blear-eyed, and vulgar, with thin, loosely jointed

legs and bent shoulders, he looked his reputation, — the terror of the neighborhood.

Nobody tried to understand the family. The
nearest neighbors, generally reliable in such
cases, could give no clear description of its members, for they never entered his door. They all
agreed, however, upon one fact, — that the tall
girl who worked in the factory, and who had
come home three years before to nurse another
baby, — this time her own, — was Hutchins's
only daughter.

Outside this battered wreck of a home, with
its frowzy inmates, Hutchins's only possessions
were a pair of lean, half-fed oxen who gained
a scanty living by nibbling at the patches of
grass which grew along the country road. Now
and then in the haying season, or when the
heavy timber was hauled to the mill, or the
road commissioners repaired the highway, their
owner would yoke them to a sun-bleached, unpainted cart as shaky as himself. This combi-
nation in the twilight, when his day's work was
done, made a gruesome picture, as it stumbled
down the steep wood road that led by one side
of my house, on the way to his own. He never
walked by the head of his oxen, as did most
countrymen, but always propped himself up in
his cart, his slouching, swaying figure outlined

against the sky, his thin legs hanging below the tailboard. When the children, guessing his condition, — the hire of the cart was always left in the tavern at the fork of the road, — called jeeringly at him, he would slide off the board and begin to throw stones. When my dog ran out, he would coax him near and then lash him with his whip. These idiosyncrasies did not endear him to his neighbors.

I have always had a sympathy for the man who is down, and so, when I met Hutchins, I always said "Good-morning" as pleasantly as I could. I never remember having said much else, nor that he ever made any other reply than a nod of his head or a short "Mornin'" hissed out between his teeth, as if the effort hurt him.

The road to my work ran by Hutchins's gate, and there, one morning, for the first time, I saw the little golden-haired grandchild who had furnished the winter nights' gossip for three years past.

When this day I stopped and spoke to the child, Hutchins slouched out from his door, called to her mother, and when the child cried and started towards me, caught up a stick angrily. Something in her face, or perhaps mine, stopped him, for when she lifted up her dim-

152

pled fingers and ran towards me, he softened and walked sullenly away.

Little by little the child and I became fast friends. She would toddle out to watch for me when I passed by in the morning, her hair flying in the wind. Sometimes, too, she would thrust her chubby sunburned hand through the broken palings and toss out a gay-colored hollyhock that blossomed low enough on its stalk for her to reach.

As the friendship grew, it ripened into an intimacy that finally culminated in her walking with me one day as far as the little bridge over the brook. These confidential relations seemed to impart their flavor to the rest of the family. I noticed that my little friend seemed less untidy, and one morning her outcast of a mother, hearing my voice, put a clean apron over her own head, thus recognizing the unkempt condition of her hair. As for Hutchins, although he never offered to speak first, he would somehow manage to have his hat in his hand when I approached, — his best attempt at a courtesy. If, however, he held me in any different esteem from the rest of his neighbors, or rather if he hated me the less, there was nothing in his manner to show it, except the slight evidences I have indicated.

HUTCHINS

When I lost my setter dog, search was made
in the village, and up and down the highway as
far as the stage went. The farmers, of course,
accused Hutchins. Everything from the robbing
of a hen-roost to the big burglary of the county
bank was laid at his door. At first I was a little
suspicious, and to test his knowledge of my loss
offered a reward. A week later I found the dog
tied to my door, and the next day learned from
my foreman that the poor fellow had followed
a gunner, and that Hutchins, hearing of it, had
walked twelve miles to the next village to bring
him back. When I taxed him with it he made
no answer, and when I handed him the reward
he dropped the bank-note on the ground and
lounged off whistling.

Winter came, and my work was still unfinished. Affairs at Hutchins's were unchanged.
The house perhaps looked a little more tumbled-
down, — the gable ends, porch, and sloping roof
hugging the big chimney the closer, as if they
feared the coming cold. The neighbors still
avoided the place, the women pretending not to
see the daughter when she passed, and the men
leering at her when they dared.

As for the daughter, my acquaintance with
her had never extended beyond a word now
and then about the child, which was al-

ways answered in a half-frightened, shrinking way.

One blustering night — it was the last week in December — I was sitting in my room alone studying some plans of a cofferdam for the better protection of a submarine foundation I was building, when there came a sharp knock at the outer door. I expected one of my men, and, catching up the lamp, shot back the bolt and raised the light aloft. A gust of snow chilled my face, nearly extinguishing the flame. Outside the snow lay in drifts, the lower branches of the cedars being half buried, while the stretch to the lower gate was an unbroken sheet of white. Around the corner of the porch my eyes caught the marks of a straggling, uneven footstep; and beyond, hurrying over the lower fence, I could barely distinguish the outline of a shrunken, shambling figure. It was Hutchins.

Stooping over to bring in the mat, now wet with snow, my mind filled with the strange visit and the stranger hurried disappearance, my hand touched a bundle tied with a cotton cord. It had evidently been laid there but a moment before. It was hard and round and wrapped in a newspaper.

I brought it to my fire and cut the string. Inside was a huge turnip the size of my two fists;

155

fastened to it was a sprig of holly. I looked up, and my eye fell on the calendar upon my mantel.

It was Christmas Eve.

TILE CLUB STORIES

AROUND THE WOOD FIRE

A BRIGHT wood fire is blazing away, whirling its sparks up the wide chimney, and warming to a comfortable temperature the group of newly arrived and half-chilled Tilers circled before it.

The polished mahogany table reflects a unique collection of pewter mugs clustered about a huge magnum of Bass.

Brightening the hearth is a cheery little brass kettle humming away all by itself, and puffing tiny jets of white steam from under its restless lid.

As each member enters the cosey room he is greeted with the customary shout of welcome. These shouts vary from a dismal groan to a chorus. Sometimes snatches of old songs with new words are interwoven with the Tiler's name, and often without rhyme or reason.

Why, for instance, the Terrapin should always be saluted with the refrain, —

" Oh, poor Terrapin !   Oh, poor Terrapin !
                    FISH ! "

the last word in a stentorian chorus, no mortal

man knows; and yet no sooner does the smiling face and sand-papered head of that worthy reptiler darken the door than every member in the room joins in that piscatorial chorus.

The Terrapin invariably stops, assumes an air of interest, listens eagerly with his hand shading his ears, as if it was the melody his soul most loved, and then, when it is all over, gravely pours himself a bumper and drinks in silence.

Again the sound of the bell tinkling down the narrow passageway comes up from its subterranean opening. An overcoat is thrown at a Tiler, a hat not his own is forced over his eyes, and he is unceremoniously hustled into the cold world, — that is, into the snow-covered garden to open the outer gate. In a moment he returns, letting in a great gust of fresh, crisp air and a brother Tiler, who is of course welcomed as usual. It proves to be Briareus. He is in a state of wrath.

There had been a meeting at the Academy, and the aged fossils and young fungi who formed the geological and botanical collection which enriched that institution had advanced ideas so utterly at variance with the established code of the Tenth Street Munich School that Briareus had left in disgust.

THE OWL, THE MARINE AND CADMIUM AT WORK.

"What do you think, Tilers, of old Umber asserting that if Velasquez had lived to-day, he could not earn a decent living as a third-rate portrait painter?"

"Think he told the truth," cut in Cadmium, an ardent admirer of the great Spaniard. "But posterity will do *us* justice."

At this reply the Haggis broke out into a prolonged Oho! in which the Club joined. When order was restored, — that is, when the steady thump of the butt end of the Griffin's carving-knife had drowned all other sounds, — its possessor remarked that Cadmium's opinion reminded him of the distinguished Anglo-American painter with the single eyeglass, the white top-lock, and the tuneful name, who, on being approached in the Royal Academy by an enthusiastic Briton with the remark, "Oh, sir; when I see your pictures, I say to myself there are only two masters, — Velasquez and you," replied, "Too true, dear boy; but why drag in Velasquez?"

While this raillery proceeds, a group of Tilers, oblivious to the noise, have their heads together at the upper end of the table listening to the Saint, who is giving the Builder and the Bishop a description of his new alto-relievo.

Farther along, seated upon the old settle between the open fireplace and the hob, are the Terrapin and the Hawk, discussing the latest results in color-printing.

The Hawk advances the theory that wood-engraving is as dead as Julius Cæsar and copperplate, and that hereafter it will be one, two, three, and it is done !

" Just think of something pleasant, my dear, and keep still. Before you can wink your eye you have the girl's head which Terrapin finished yesterday photographed from the original canvas on a sheet of zinc, slapped on a Hoe press, and by sundown an edition of fifty thousand copies is in the hands of the newsboys. ' Here 's your horiginal 'ead by the famous hartist, B. Terrapin, five cents,' accompanied by an editorial paragraph congratulating the public on the publication, and calling particular attention to the fact that the enterprise of the journal will be appreciated when it is known that at the present writing the paint is not dry on the Terrapin's canvas."

" Order ! " yells the Catgut. " Stop that infernal din in the corner, and you fellows drop that art stuff and listen to a sonata that will melt your soul into honey."

Joe, the sable attendant, is already lighting the candles and bringing out the music stands.

Catgut proceeds to undress his violin, stripping off its overhauls of green baize, tightens up his bow, caulks the cavity between his Adam's apple and his chin with his handkerchief, and lays lovingly against it his old Cremona. Meanwhile the Husk runs his fingers lightly over the keys of the piano, a sharp rap follows from Catgut's bow, and a dead silence falls upon the noisy room. They know too well the exquisite touch of that wrist and finger to spoil a single harmony.

As the heavenly melodies of Beethoven's " Kreutzer Sonata " float through the room, the occupants settle themselves in their easy chairs, listening quietly, puffing silently, and occasionally reaching for a short pull at the pewter mugs, which are within the grasp of every man's hand. The spell conjured so deftly by the Catgut has had its effect. They urge him to continue. Now they want Schumann's " Träumerei."

But the Catgut pleads a devouring thirst, and the Husk says he has not eaten anything "for fourteen days, so help him," and insists on Joe broiling him a kidney before he touches another ivory. This subterfuge is met with much opposition. In fact, the demand is considered farcical. Music they want and will have.

However, before brute force is used, another

shout of welcome goes up, and the big burly form of the Baritone fills the half-open door. He has arrived in the nick of time. In an instant he is unceremoniously denuded of his overcoat and hat, shot into a seat facing the piano, and ordered to sing without further delay an old Bedouin love song, greatly prized and oft repeated, under pain of having the top of his pewter mug roofed over and forever sealed and he go dry the balance of his life.

The Baritone is the *beau idéal* of the Club. He has a voice once heard never forgotten. It is as delicious as a 'cello and strong as a full brass band, and has a quality of lifting one up into midair by his waistband and holding him out at arm's length. He does full credit to his reputation, and is for the hundredth time vociferously applauded.

As the last words of the beautiful song die away, a shout of laughter is heard from around the table. In an instant the humor of the room has changed. Polyphemus is telling of a night he had at the Garrick. Then the Owl follows with one of Uncle Remus's " reminuisances," as he calls them ; and then story after story is fired off in quick succession, reminding one of a target company at practice.

Soon the talk drifts into studio gossip, and the

history of past, present, and future "pot-boil-
ers" is told and commented upon. Later on the
Pagan heaves a deep sigh and discourses of
Capri, and of a certain dark-eyed girl who filled
his heart and emptied his pocket in the old stu-
dent days.

"Is that why you painted the 'Sibyl'?"
said Briareus.

"The same, my boy."

"But now tell me, Briareus," said the Pagan, "how you came to paint that garden with
the girl in the hammock. Whose girl was she,
anyhow? Yours, or the natty fellow's in the
flannel suit?"

"Neither, you heathen. She was from one
of the provinces. Her father was an officer in
the French army, and her mother an invalid
trying the bracing air of the Holland coast.
Their apartments joined mine, and, like mine,
opened upon a delightful garden. Our acquaintance began to blossom through the slats of the
dividing fence, ripened on the front steps, and
flourished vigorously until she was gathered into
a hammock under one of my trees. The young
fellow in flannel was simply a brother brush,
who passed a few days with me on his way to
Venice."

"All true," said the Owl. "I remember the

old garden, and the fence, and the tree. I examined them carefully by the light of a kerosene lamp one night last summer. I had been in Haarlem only one hour when I heard from the porter of the hotel that Mynheer Briareus was stopping at Zandvoort, a few miles distant.

"I ordered a trap, drove six miles through a sand heap, arrived after dark, borrowed a lantern and a Dutchman, groped my way down crooked lanes, over sand-dunes and grass-tufted hillocks, to a long low row of whitewashed houses, pulled a bell, strode past a pretty white-capped fish-girl, through a narrow hall, and halted at the open door of a low bedroom.

"Briareus was in his shirt-sleeves, his back to me, writing a letter. If some one had asked him at that moment where was the Owl, he would have said three thousand miles away, and wagered a fortune on the truth of his statement.

"'Come in off that wet grass,' I shouted suddenly. It would have done you good to have seen him jump.

"'By the Great Horn Spoon,' he cried; 'there is but one man on the globe who uses that expression, and' —

"'I am he, old man,' said I, falling into his outstretched arms."

"But about that garden and the girl," inquired the Bone.

"Oh, he showed me the picture just commenced, and the outline of the girl; and as I returned that night to Haarlem, insisted on my examining the garden by lamplight."

"Did n't show you the girl, did he?" said Cadmium.

"No, only the outline."

"Of course not," muttered the Haggis. "That's as near as anybody ever gets to Briareus's girls."

"Or he, either — with a brush," added Polyphemus.

"Now tell us why you painted the Bridge, Owl?" said the Marine. "Was there nothing else for you around this metropolis but this great ugly pile of masonry and dingy old houses underneath?"

"Plenty of them, my boy; but one afternoon I came out of Harper's just at twilight, crossed the square, and caught sight of this great mass looming up against the evening sky. I was in search of a subject for our exhibition. This magnificent structure seemed to convey to me the impression of the genius of the nineteenth century towering above the eighteenth. The next day I looked the subject over carefully, dropped into a corner grocery, borrowed a blue lead pencil and a sheet of brown paper, mounted the steps of the elevated road, made my first outline composition, which I never afterwards altered, returned the next day with a fifty-inch canvas and an easel, and spent the succeeding eight on the platform. It was early in December, and when I finished I was stiff as an icicle and half frozen through."

"Served you right," said Cadmium. "No business to paint out of doors. What you wanted was your brown paper sketch and your impression. If you had waited those eight days and let it simmer in your brain, it would have amounted to something."

"Picture might, brain never would," said Polyphemus.

"That's bosh, Cadmium, and you know it," said the Marine, famous for his outdoor work. "To paint nature truthfully you must surprise it, catching it on the wing, not potter over it day after day until you have worked all the 'go' out of it. The fact is, it takes two men to produce a picture, — one to paint it, and the other to kill him when he has done enough."

"Talks like an art critic," said Polyphemus, who sustained that relation to the outside public.

"And with as little common sense," said the Bishop, who had had a recent picture slashed into mince-meat by that Argus-eyed gentleman the week before, and who still felt a little sore over it.

"How about Corot and Daubigny and Millet," said Briareus. "Do you suppose they sat outdoors with the thermometer at par or zero, and pegged away in the rain and heat?"

"Certainly, my boy," said the Marine. "That is just what they did do, and did it every day they could drag their bones out into the air. Corot spent three years of his life mastering one effect of silvery light behind gray-green foliage, and then wanted to bury himself in a self-digged hole in the ground because he had not reproduced all there was in it. But you fellows claim to paint the earth, and think you do it. Interiors, still life, landscape, figures, portraits, genre, marines. You do them all. If you don't see what you want, ask for it. That is your modern doctrine to the public."

"Will somebody open the window and let the Marine fly out?" said Haggis.

"Shoo fly, don't bodder me," broke in the Husk; and in another minute the old negro chorus, taken up by nearly every member in the room, drowned all other sounds, and cut

169

short the Marine's caustic reply and the discussion.

"Kidney ready, sir." This fact had been apparent to the whole room for some time, and also the fact that Joe, who held the toothsome morsel on a hot plate, had been beating Juba with his foot and keeping time with his head to the melody.

The Husk pounced upon it, dusted it with cayenne, plunged his beak into the great pewter tankard (the loving cup of the Club), and then said he was now ready for another sonata.

But the room was no longer music-mad; again had its humor changed.

It was instantly voted to stand the Husk on his head in the back garden in the snow, and erect the Catgut's violin over him as a tombstone, if he sounded another note.

"Hold on, Bulgarian; I am going your way," called out the Saint from his end of the room, waking up to consciousness and the hour, after a prolonged argument with the Builder as to the original condition of the Milo, and as to whether the Venus had held her arms up or down in the land of her birth.

The Bulgarian waited, then wrapped his overcoat about him, fastened over his ears an astrachan that had done good service under Skobeleff, said "How," and, linking his arm in the Saint's, disappeared through the door.

Then the Horsehair, Catgut, and Builder followed, and soon the cosey room contained only the Pagan, the Owl, the Haggis, the Bone, and a few others.

The hands of the clock in the tall tower near by pointed to midnight.

CLUB CHESTNUTS WARMED OVER

FILL that kettle with water, Polyphemus, and brew us a punch. I have a story to tell."

The Owl waited until the water ran over the hob, and a lemon and flagon and a few lumps of sugar had added a savory flavor to the clouds of smoke drifting in horizontal lines about the room, then refilled his pipe, balanced his feet on the fender, looked around quietly to see that everybody was comfortable, and began as follows : —

THE OWL'S STORY

One afternoon about sundown I arrived at a small town in the western part of the island of Cuba called Artimeza. It consisted of a long rambling street, flanked on either side with palms, at one end of which was a low rickety posada offering scanty accommodation to man and mule. Being a loyal Tiler I thirsted for a glass of beer, and being ignorant of the name it bore in Spanish, I was in a fair way of going without it, when a pale, dark-eyed young Cuban stepped forward, opened up a conversation with good English and a bottle of Bass with a poor corkscrew, and sat down with me to share both. We spent the evening together, and the result was that he promised to breakfast with me at the posada in the morning, provided I would visit his uncle's plantation later the same day.

The next morning before I finished dressing the courtyard of the posada was invaded by a cavalcade, consisting of a volante drawn by two mules, with their riders, two saddle-horses, and three negro attendants.

Don Hacher explained that he had neglected to inquire of me whether I would ride or drive, and so, with true Cuban politeness, he had brought conveniences for both luxuries. I selected the saddle.

After a wretched breakfast, consisting of an India-rubber chicken stewed in garlic and seasoned with red peppers, we took up our line of march through a tropical country rich in sugar and tobacco, until we reached the corner of a stone wall.

" The beginning of my uncle's plantation," said Don Hacher. Proceeding along this wall for a mile, we rode up a broad double-rowed avenue of royal palms, and halted at a hacienda of wide piazzas, rich flowering tropical plants, and the usual collection of hammocks, birds, and easy chairs, common to all plantations of its class.

The uncle proved to be equally agreeable, was delighted to meet a stranger from beyond the sea, and immediately placed his fortune, his house, and his breakfast at my disposal.

My struggle with the chicken prevented my accepting the last, his fortune I did not want, and so I contented myself with examining his house, — the second item of his generosity.

It was large, well furnished, plentifully supplied with rocking-chairs, and presided over by a remarkably pretty woman, with lustrous black eyes. This was his second wife, and presumably not included in the gift. While coffee was being served, my friend gave me a short history of the plantation.

It was the largest in the vicinity ; had in former times been famous for its coffee yield, but was now given over to the cultivation of sugar.

Since the revolution its revenues had been greatly curtailed, only a portion of the estate tilled, and many of the buildings, including a great distillery, a hospital, and slave prison, abandoned. Seeing me greatly interested in a portrait which covered a panel in the room, he said, lowering his voice and motioning to his uncle, —

"It is his grandfather. He was, as you see, an officer in the German army, and served under Frederick the Great."

When the extreme heat of the day had passed, Don Hacher offered to show me the estate. We went alone.

The distillery, part of which was underground, was in ruins. The floor was covered with green mould, the walls reeking with slime and ooze ; the casks, held together only by their rusty iron hoops, were rotted and worm-eaten, and the great retorts and furnaces encrusted with rank vegetation. It was the home of the lizard and centipede. Not destroyed by violence or accident, but by the decay of the grave.

The prison quarters were in but little better repair. Manacles half eaten with rust were hanging from the cobwebbed beams, and the rude wooden stocks were broken and useless.

"What is this great stone building ? " I asked, finding that Don Hacher passed it without remark.

"It was once used as a hospital. The crack which you see from the roof downwards was the mark left by an earthquake several years ago."

" Can I go inside ? "

He hesitated, pushed open a swinging-door, and discovered a flight of circular stone steps, protected by a light iron railing, winding up lighthouse fashion.

" Where does this lead ? "

Don Hacher did not reply, and seemed absorbed in thought. Then he turned to me, and said, —

" As you are a stranger and a gentleman, I will show you."

He walked to the corner of the building, called a negro, gave him an order in Spanish, waited until he returned with a bunch of keys, delayed until he was again out of sight, shut carefully the swinging-door behind us, and preceded me up the winding stairs.

A draught of hot air from a grated window met me at the landing, at one end of which was a corridor terminating in a wooden door heavily barred. The casing and lock were covered with cobwebs, and it was difficult to find the keyhole under the layers of dead spiders and insects. It had evidently remained so many years.

Don Hacher turned the key, swung around

176

the wooden bar, pressed his weight against the door, and forced it open.

A great cloud of black dust arose, nearly suffocating us.

When it settled, I found myself in a room about a hundred feet long, wide and high in proportion, and lighted by three large iron-grated windows without glass.

The ceiling, once richly frescoed, was now stained and blistered by exposure to storm and wind beating through the open gratings. Heaped up over the floor and into the corners and against the side walls, in some places literally ankle deep, were great drifts of dust and débris, consisting of the dried feathered-skeletons of dead birds, lizards, bats, beetles, and other insects.

The walls were lined on all four sides with wooden cases extending to the ceiling, and their shelves were loaded down with a solid mass of books.

Books everywhere, — on the window-sills, bleached and half rotten ; on the floor, buried in black dust-drifts ; in the corners, on shelves on small tables and ledges, — nothing but books, manuscripts, charts, and folios.

I examined their titles closely. They were German, French, English, and Spanish publications, denoting early editions of Shakespeare in vellum and leather, voyages of Bruce and Cook in calf, editions of Homer, Æschylus, Plato, Plutarch, and others of the classics in fine bindings, — all showing the library of a man of extensive learning, wide reading, and unusual cultivation.

My eye lighted on an edition of Don Quixote in two volumes superbly bound in white leather, now rich and yellow with age. As I lifted one volume from the shelf the backs came apart in my hands. The imprint showed that these were the original first editions, volume one of which was published in 1605 and volume two exactly ten years later. On the title-page of the second volume was written in Spanish, "Cervantes and Shakespeare meet in heaven this day, April 23, 1616."

In amazement I turned to speak to Hacher. He had crossed the room and was standing by a large table. He was watching me curiously.

"See," he said, pointing to the table and a chair beside it, "here is where he studied and worked, and wore his life away."

I drew closer. The top, once green velvet, was covered with layers of grime and dust. A dead bat swarming with vermin lay upon an unfinished manuscript. The wooden inkstand, bristling with quills, was a mass of tangled webs and dead flies. Scattered about were seals, some pieces of faded tape, a candlestick without a candle, a rusted knife, and the usual knickknacks and trifles.

"Don Hacher, what is the meaning of this? Whose library was it?" I asked.

He looked at me earnestly, made no reply, and shook his head. Then turned abruptly, replaced carefully the volume I held in my hand, conducted me to the door, barred and locked it, and preceded me silently downstairs and out into the blinding sunlight.

For some time we walked together in silence. When we neared the hacienda he stopped, looked me steadily in the eye, laid his hand on my shoulder, pointed in the direction of his uncle, and, placing his fingers to his lips, said, —

"Remember!"

"I will, Hacher; but answer me one question. Why is this library closed?"

"I cannot," he said firmly. "It is a mystery."

"Did you never find out?" inquired the Haggis.

"Never," replied the Owl. "I could not ask the uncle. Hacher had closed the conversation so far as he was concerned, nobody else

179

spoke English, and I left for Havana the next day."

" Belonged to the old cock whose portrait hung on the wall," suggested the Pagan.

"And was ordered kept closed in his will under forfeiture of the estate," added the Boarder, who is something of a lawyer.

" Anything you please, boys. I have given you every scrap of information I own," said the Owl, lighting a cigarette and refilling his glass.

"Most extraordinary," said the Bone, who is the bookworm of the Club. " What was the date of the Quixote ? Bound in *white* leather, too. Must have been the very first edition."

Then the Haggis, who had recently returned from a West Indian cruise in a friend's yacht, related some experiences at Martinique, in which some dusky brown girls, dressed in full suits of silver bangles, were thoroughly mixed up at a diving match with a boat's crew which he commanded.

"I know the girls," put in the Griffin, " regular bronze Venuses, every one of them. Dive like ducks — catch a dime quicker than a trout. But, speaking of Cuba, I ran amuck one Sunday afternoon in Matanzas which I won't forget in a hurry."

CLUB CHESTNUTS WARMED OVER

THE GRIFFIN'S STORY

Running up from the Bella Mar, or Beautiful Sea of Matanzas, is a narrow canal, leading to the slaughter-houses of the city. Every morning and evening, at sunrise and sundown, a procession of sharks moves up from the sea, glides through this canal, feeds on the offal, and returns. It is one of the sights of the place, and I took it in.

That I am alive to-day to tell of it only proves the doctrine of the "survival of the fittest" and of the "devil take the hindmost." I was in a small boat following these sharks and watching their fins cut through the water, when I heard the sound of beating tom-toms on my right, accompanying the weird, nervous, irritating, jerky music of the African dance. I knew the sound instantly, for I had frequently heard it in Morocco, and once saw such a performance in Tunis.

It flashed over me all at once that many of these negroes in Matanzas were victims of the slave-trade and must still keep up their old customs. In an instant I had moored the skiff and began following up the sound. Soon I reached a row of low whitewashed houses, one of which was surrounded by a group of men and women,

—all negroes, and all decked out in their war-
paint of artificial flowers and gay colored rib-
bons.

Edging through the throng, I caught a glimpse
of the inside of the dancing-room through the
low window.

On the floor, backed against the rear wall,
sat four negroes. This was the band. One was
beating a kettle-drum, another a small circular
brass gong, a third held a long two-stringed instrument something like a Chinese guitar, the
strings of which he rubbed with a piece of bone
well rosined, and the fourth slapped with the
flat of his hand the sides of a rude-looking drum
made like a barrel, except that its top and bottom were covered with dried cowhide. Such
instruments are quite common anywhere on
the north or west coast of Africa.

The other three sides of the room were packed
full of negroes, young and old, evidently under
the influence of the music, rocking themselves
backward and forward, keeping time with their
hands, and beating their foreheads. In the middle of the floor was a negro wench dressed in
what was once a stiff-starched white dress, now
a limp and bedraggled gown. The perspiration was dropping from her face and arms, her
eyes were red and protruding, her mouth open,

and she panting from the exhaustion of the dance.

Opposite her and following every motion, now imitating and now leading in a new step, was a bullet-headed young negro dancing bare-footed. He, too, was nearly used up. The music, however, seemed to pump new life into them. When the girl would reel and stagger, a fresh outburst of the band would buoy her up and save her from falling. But it was evident that the pace was too steep. Suddenly I saw her throw up her arms, clutch at the air with her fingers, and fall headlong on the floor.

A yell went up like a Comanche war-whoop, the girl was picked up, hurried into the adjoining room, laid on the floor to cool off and come to, and the floor was cleared for a fresh couple.

This gave me a chance to slip through the door and into one corner of the room, where I could watch the next figure more closely. The fact was, I had at home an unfinished canvas, which I had begun in Tangier, showing an Arab encampment. I wanted to introduce a group of dancing figures in the foreground, and this seemed an admirable opportunity to study them. It certainly possessed all the elements of a barbaric dance.

The sylph that stepped out next was a thin,

angular, rawboned young negress, whose kinky hair was twisted into little pigtails, each one of which was bound with a different colored ribbon. Clinging to her lank figure was a bright calico dress trimmed with paper flowers. Covering her feet, which were about the size of lemon boxes, were white kid slippers. These she flapped on the floor like a flail.

She began by walking around in a circle, flirting a red silk handkerchief in the faces of the sitting and kneeling negroes and challenging them to dance.

Presently one shot up like a jack-in-the-box, seized the handkerchief, and the fun began.

Hardly had he moved a dozen paces when a negress next me gave a piercing scream, and the next instant the head and shoulders of the most devilish looking negro you ever saw were thrust through the window. The girl saw him, gave a shriek, turned a light green, and bolted through the rear door. Her companion whipped out a murderous-looking dirk, and backed into my corner with his legs spanning my knees.

Before I could move, the first negro (who I found afterwards was the lover of the girl) jumped through the window and made a spring at the throat of the colored gentleman who was using me as a cushion. The first slash he gave

184

came within six inches of my head, the next sliced down the dancer's arm, ripping open his shirt and spattering the wall with blood.

I looked up through a mass of arms waving chairs, razors, knives, and clubs, watched my chance, gathered myself for a spring, cleared the window at a bound, and made a bee-line for my boat. It was the closest shave I ever had. I can see now that ugly sickle-shaped dirk sweeping around my head. It gives me a cold shiver every time I think of it.

The Griffin got up, poured a thimbleful from the flagon, drank it, and moved one seat nearer the fire.

The Tilers also hitched their chairs closer, and the Bone whispered to the Pagan that the story was good enough to print, and should not be wasted on ears turned upside down.

Then the Builder followed with an adventure near Athens, resulting in the loss of some precious manuscripts collected at great cost of purse and risk of limb, and asked Briareus if he knew Greece.

" No, it is not in the line of my wanderings ; but if you would like to hear about an adventure I had in Madrid some time since, I will recall it for you."

CLUB CHESTNUTS WARMED OVER

BRIAREUS'S STORY

Three years ago I was in Madrid studying Velasquez. It was the summer I made those copies of the Actor and Æsopus.

One afternoon I left the gallery, strolled down the Prado, and lounged into a café. The first man I met was Minton, a brother brush from Boston. While we were taking our coffee, I overheard a conversation at the next table. A Spaniard was describing how he had deliberately tortured a dog to death merely to see his dying agony. It seemed so incredible to me that any human being could be so cruel that, regardless of my friend's warning, I left my seat, crossed to the Spaniard's table, and, smothering my indignation, asked him in French if he was a scientist or surgeon.

" No, señor."

" Why, then, did you torture the dog ? " I demanded angrily.

" Patience, señor. He was mine. Can I not do as I please with my own dog without your permission ? "

Before I could reply Minton interfered, dragged me into the street, and hurried me away to another café.

The next morning, while passing through a

crooked street near the Puerta del Sol, I was startled at seeing a white spaniel thrown from a doorway. He landed almost at my feet, and lay writhing and howling with pain.

In an instant all my anger of the previous afternoon came over me with a rush. "Here's another brutal Spaniard," I said to myself. "The poor fellow's agony shall be short anyhow." Reaching down, I struck him between the ears with the heavy end of my cane, crushing in his skull. He rolled over dead.

The next moment I was confronted by a frowzy-headed Spaniard, literally livid with rage. He could hardly keep his hands from my throat. Through his ravings I gathered the information that he owned the dog and wanted to know why I had killed him.

I saw it was hopeless, with my limited knowledge of Spanish, to explain to this maniac all my philanthropic reasons for quickly ending the poor creature's misery, and so I merely confined myself to insisting that he should immediately accompany me to a neighboring café, where I knew a Spanish friend who spoke English. Finally he agreed to go. On the way I turned over in my mind just what I would say to him. When we reached the café, my friend was not in. Then I bethought me of the Lega-

187

tion but a few squares distant. But my lunatic would not budge. What he wanted was an apology, a new dog, or blood, and he wanted it right away.

I drew out my card, inscribed upon it my address, and added the hour at which I would receive him or his second. He tucked it carefully away in his vest pocket, raised his hat, and disappeared around the corner.

I hunted up Minton and posted him on the situation. He looked very grave and considered it critical.

Promptly at seven P. M. a card was brought me on a tray, bearing this inscription : —

DON IGNACIO LAVANDEYRA

The Don followed the tray. He was still hot, but cool enough to be handled without a pair of tongs.

Minton opened the ball. He explained that I was a renowned philanthropist, dearly loved dogs, and could not stand seeing one abused and tortured.

188

"Ah! how very gentle is this American. He does not like to see the dog hurt by his master, and so he cracks his skull himself, eh?"

"Certainly," said Minton. "So that you could no longer torture him."

"Me! I torture him? I have reared him, señor, from a baby dog. Every day I feed him three times. He sleeps on my bed at night. For a year he has had fits. Then he goes into the street and lies down. In five minutes they are gone. Then he comes to me again."

"You need n't laugh, boys. I have n't gotten over it yet. I did n't mind apologizing to Don Ignacio a bit, and I must say he took it very well and behaved very handsomely about it. It was bad enough to have murdered the poor animal; it was worse to see Minton rolling over on the floor, and holding his sides and laughing himself sore. Ever since that day when he sees me, he pulls out an imaginary card and goes through a pantomime with an invisible dog and a walking stick. Sometimes I want to brain him on the spot."

BÄADER

I WAS sitting in the shadow of Mme. Poulard's delightful inn at St. Michel when I first
saw Bäader. Dinner had been served, and I had
helped to pay for my portion by tacking a sketch
on the wall behind the chair of the hostess.
This high valuation was not intended as a special compliment to me, the wall being already
covered with similar souvenirs from the sketch-
books of half the painters in Europe.

Bäader — he pronounced it Bayder — had at
that moment arrived in answer to a telegram
from the governor, who the night before, in a
moment of desperation, had telegraphed the proprietor of his hotel in Paris, "Send me a courier at once who knows Normandy and speaks
English." The bareheaded man who, hat in
hand, was at this moment bowing so obsequi-
ously to the governor, was the person who had
arrived in response. He was short and thickset, and perfectly bald on the top of his head in
a small spot, friar-fashion. He glistened with
perspiration that collected near the hatline, and

escaped in two streams, drowning locks of black
hair covering each temple, stranding them like
wet grass on his cheekbones below. His full
face was clean-shaven, smug, and persuasive,
and framed two shoe-button eyes that, while
sharp and alert, lacked neither humor nor tenderness.

He wore a pair of new green kid gloves, was
dressed in a brown cloth coat bound with a
braid of several different shades, showing different dates of repair, and surmounted by a velvet
collar of the same date as the coat. His trousers were of a nondescript gray, and flapped
about a pair of brand-new gaiters, evidently
purchased for the occasion, and, from the numerous positions assumed while he talked, evidently one size too small.

His hat — the judicious use of which added
such warmth, color, and picturesqueness to his
style of delivery, now pressed to his chest, now
raised aloft, now debased to the cobbles — had
once had some dignity and proportions. Con-
tinual maltreatment had long since taken all the
gay and frolicsome curl out of its brim, while
the crown had so often collapsed that the scars
of ill-usage were visible upon it. And yet at a
distance this relic of a former fashion, as handled by Bäader, — it was so continually in his

grasp and so seldom on his head, that you could never say it was worn, — this hat, brushed, polished, and finally slicked by its owner to a state slightly confusing as to whether it were made of polished iron or silk, was really a very gay and attractive affair.

It was easy to see that the person before me had spared neither skill, time, nor expense to make as favorable an impression on his possible employers as lay in his power.

"At ze moment of ze arrival of ze dépêche télégraphique," Bäader continued, "I was in ze office of monsieur ze propriétaire. It was at ze conclusion of some arrangement commercial, when mon ami ze propriétaire say to me: 'Bäader, it is ze abandoned season in Paris. Why not arrange for ze gentlemen in Normandy? The number of francs a day will be at least'" — here Bäader scrutinized carefully the governor's face — "'at least to ze amount of ten' — is it not so, messieurs? Of course," noting a slight contraction of the eyebrows, "if ze service was of long time, and to ze most far-away point, some abatement could be posseeble. If, par exemple, it was to St. Malo, St. Servan, Paramé, Cancale spéciale, Dieppe petite, Dinard, and ze others, ze sum of nine francs would be quite sufficient."

The governor had never heard Dieppe called "petite" nor Cancale "spéciale," and said so, lifting his eyebrows inquiringly. Bäader did not waver. "But if messieurs pretend a much smaller route and of few days, say to St. Michel, Paramé, and Cancale," — here the governor's brow relaxed again, — "then it was impossee-ble, — if messieurs will pardon, — quite impos-seeble for less zan ten francs."

So the price was agreed upon, and the hat, now with a decided metallic sheen, once more swept the cobblestones of the courtyard. The ceremony being over, its owner then drew off the green kid gloves, folded them flat on his knee, guided them into the inside pocket of the brown coat with the assorted bindings as care-fully as if they had been his letter of credit, and declared himself at our service.

It was when he had been installed as custo-dian not only of our hand luggage, but to a cer-tain extent of our bank accounts and persons for some days, that he urged upon the governor the advisability of our at once proceeding to Cancale, or Cancale spéciale, as he insisted on calling it. I immediately added my own voice to his pleadings, arguing that Cancale must cer-tainly be on the sea. That, from my recollec-tion of numerous water-colors and black-and-whites labelled in the catalogue, "Coast near Cancale," and the like, I was sure there must be the customary fish-girls, with shrimp-nets carried gracefully over one shoulder, to say nothing of brawny-chested fishermen with flat, rimless caps, having the usual little round button on top.

The governor, however, was obdurate. He had a way of being obdurate when anything irritated him, and Bäader began to be one of these things. Cancale might be all very well for me, but how about the hotel for him, who had nothing to do, no pictures to paint? He had passed that time in his life when he could sleep under a boat with water pouring down the back of his neck through a tarpaulin full of holes.

"Ze hotel, messieurs! Imagine! Is it posseeble that monsieur imagine for one moment that Bäader would arrange such annoyances? I remember ze hotel quite easily. It is not like, of course, ze Grand Hôtel of Paris, but it is simple, clean, ze cuisine superb, and ze apartment fine and hospitable. Remembare, it is Bäader."

"And the baths?" broke out the governor savagely.

Bäader's face was a study; a pained, deprecating expression passed over it as he uncovered his head, his glazed headpiece glistening in the sun.

" Baths, monsieur — and ze water of ze sea everywhere ? "

These assurances of future comfort were not overburdened with details, but they served to satisfy and calm the governor, I pleading, meanwhile, that Bäader had always proved himself a man of resource, quite ready when required with either a meal or an answer.

So we started for Cancale.

On the way our courier grew more and more enthusiastic. We were travelling in a four-seated carriage, Bäader on the box, pointing out to us in English, after furtive conversations with the driver in French, the principal points of interest. With many flourishes he led us to Paramé, one of those Normandy cities which consist of a huge hotel with enormous piazzas, a beach ten miles from the sea, and a small so-called fishing-village as a sort of marine attachment. To give a realistic touch, a lone boat is always being tarred somewhere down at the end of one of its toy streets, two or three donkey-carts and donkeys add an air of picturesqueness, and the usual number of children with red pails and shovels dig in the sand of the roadside. All the fish that are sold come from the next town. It was too early in the season when we reached there for girls in sabots and white caps, the tide from Paris not having set in. The governor hailed it with delight. " Why the devil did n't you tell me about this place before ? Here we have been fooling away our time."

" But it is only Paramé, monsieur," with an accent on the " only " and a lifting of the hands. " Cancale spéciale will charm you ; ze coast it is so immediately flat, and ze life of ze sea charmante. Nevare at Paramé, always at Cancale." So we drove on. The governor pacified but anxious — only succumbing at my argument that Bäader knew all Normandy thoroughly, and that an old courier like him certainly could be trusted to select a hotel.

You all know the sudden dip from the rich, flat country of Normandy down the steep cliffs to the sea. Cancale is like the rest of it. The town itself stands on the brink of a swoop to the sands ; the fishing-village proper, where the sea packs it solid in a great half moon, with a light burning on one end that on clear nights can be seen as far as Mme. Poulard's cosey dining-room at St. Michel.

One glimpse of this sea-burst tumbled me

out of the carriage, sketch-trap in hand. Bäader and the governor kept on. If the latter noticed the discrepancy between Bäader's description of the country and the actual topography, no word fell from him at the moment of departure.

From my aerie, as I worked under my white umbrella below the cliff, I could distinctly make out our travelling carriage several hundred feet below and a mile away, crawling along a road of white tape with a green selvage of trees, the governor's glazed trunk flashing behind, Bäader's silk hat burning in front. Then the little insect stopped at a white spot backed by dots of green ; a small speck broke away, and was swallowed up for a few minutes in the white dot, — doubtless Bäader to parley for rooms, — and then to my astonishment the whole insect turned and began crawling back again, growing larger every minute. All this occurred before I had half finished my outline or opened my color-box. Instantly the truth dawned upon me, — the governor was going back to Paramé. An hour, perhaps, had elapsed when Bäader, with uncovered head and beaded with perspiration, the two locks of hair hanging limp and straight, stood before me.

"What was the matter with the governor, Bäader ? No hotel after all ?"

197

"On ze contraire, pardonnez-moi, monsieur, a most excellent hotel, simple and quite of ze people, and with many patrons. Even at ze moment of arrival, a most distinguished artist, a painter of ze Salon, was with his cognac upon a table at ze entrance."

"No bath, perhaps," I remarked casually, still absorbed in my work, and with my mind at rest, now that Bäader remained with me.

"On ze contraire, monsieur, les bains are most excellent — primitive, of course, simple, and quite of ze people. But, monsieur le gouverneur is no more young. When one is no more young," — with a deprecating shrug, — "parbleu, it is imposseeble to enjoy everything. Monsieur le gouverneur, I do assure you, make ze conclusion most regretfully to return to Paramé."

I learned the next morning that he evinced every desire to drown Bäader in the surf for bringing him to such an inn, and was restrained only by the knowledge that I should miss his protection during my one night in Cancale.

"Moreover, it is ze grande fête to-night — ze fête of ze République. Zare are fireworks and illumination and music by ze municipality. It is simple, but quite of ze people. It is for zis

198

reason that I made ze effort special with monsieur le gouverneur to remain with you. Ah!
it is you, monsieur, who are so robust, so enthusiastic, so appreciative."

Here Bäader put on his hat, and I closed my
sketch-trap.

" But monsieur has not yet dined," he said
as we walked, "nor even at his hotel arrived.
Ze inn of Mme. Flamand is so very far away,
and ze ascent up ze cliffs difficile. If monsieur
will be so good, zare is a café near by where it
is quite posseeble to dine."

Relieved of the governor's constant watchfulness, Bäader became himself. He bustled about
the restaurant, called for " Cancale spéciale,"
a variety of oysters apparently entirely unknown to the landlord, and interviewed the
chef himself. In a few moments a table was
spread in a corner of the porch overlooking a
garden gay with hollyhocks, and a dinner was
ordered of broiled chicken, French rolls, some
radishes, half a dozen apricots, and a fragment
of cheese. When it was over, — Bäader had
been served in an adjoining apartment, — there
remained not the amount mentioned in a former
out-of-door feast, but sufficient to pack at least
one basket, — in this case a paper box, — the
drumsticks being stowed below, dunnaged by

two rolls, and battened down with fragments of cheese and three apricots.

"What's this for, Bäader? Have you not had enough to eat?"

Bäader's face wore its blandest smile. "On ze contraire, I have made for myself a most excellent repast; but if monsieur will consider — ze dinner is a prix fixe, and monsieur can eat it all, or it shall remain for ze propriétaire. Zis, if monsieur will for one moment attend, will be stupid extraordinaire. I have made ze investigation, and discover zat ze post départ from Cancale in one hour. How simple zen to affeex ze stamps, — only five sous, — and in ze morning, even before Mme. Bäader is out of ze bed, it is in Paris, — a souvenir from Cancale. How charmante ze surprise!"

I discovered afterward that since he had joined us Bäader's own domestic larder had been almost daily enriched with crumbs like these from Dives's table.

The fête, despite Bäader's assurances, lacked one necessary feature. There was no music. The band was away with the boats, the triangle probably cooking, the French horn and clarinet hauling seines.

But Bäader, not to be outdone by any contretemps, started off to find an old blind fellow who played an accordeon, collecting five francs of me in advance for his pay, under the plea that it was quite horrible that the young people could not dance. "While one is young, monsieur, music is ze life of ze heart."

He brought the old man back, and with a certain care and tenderness set him down on a stone bench, the sightless eyes of the poor peasant turning up to the stars as he swayed the primitive instrument back and forth. The young girls clung to Bäader's arm, and blessed him for his goodness. I forgave him his duplicity, his delight in their happiness was so genuine. Perhaps it was even better than a fête.

When, later in the evening, we arrived at Mme. Flamand's, we found her in the doorway, her brown face smiling, her white cap and apron in full relief under the glare of an old-fashioned ship's light, which hung from a rafter of the porch. Bäader inscribed my name in a much-thumbed, ink-stained register, which looked like a neglected ship's log, and then added his own. This, by the bye, Bäader never neglected. Neither did he neglect a certain little ceremony always connected with it.

After it was all over and "Moritz Bäader, Courrier et Interprète," was duly inscribed, — and in justice it must be confessed it was al-

ways clearly written with a flourish at the end
that lent it additional dignity, — Bäader would
pause for a moment, carefully balance the pen,
trying it first on his thumb-nail, and then place
two little dots of ink over the first *a*, saying,
with a certain wave of his hand, as he did so,
"For ze honor of my families, monsieur." This
peculiarity gained for him from the governor
the sobriquet of "old fly-specks."

The inn of Mme. Flamand, although less pre-
tentious than many others that had sheltered
us, was clean and comfortable, the lower deck
and companionway were freshly sanded, — the
whole house had a decidedly nautical air about
it, — and the captain's stateroom on the upper deck, a second-floor room, was large and
well lighted, although the ceiling might have
been a trifle too low for the governor, and the
bed a few inches too short.

I ascended to the upper deck, preceded by the
hostess carrying the ship's lantern, now that
the last guest had been housed for the night.
Bäader followed with a brass candlestick and a
tallow dip about the size of a lead pencil. With
the swinging open of the bedroom door, I made
a mental inventory of all the conveniences :
bed, two pillows, plenty of windows, wash-
stand, towels. Then the all-important question

recurred to me, Where had they hidden the portable tub ?

I opened the door of the locker, looked behind a sea-chest, then out of one window, expecting to see the green-painted luxury hanging by a hook or drying on a convenient roof. In some surprise I said, —

" And the bath, Bäader ? "

"Does monsieur expect to bathe at ze night ? " inquired Bäader with a lifting of his eyebrows, his face expressing a certain alarm for my safety.

" No, certainly not ; but to-morrow, when I get up."

" Ah, to-morrow ! " with a sigh of relief. " I do assure you, monsieur, zat it will be complete. At ze moment of ze déflexion of monsieur le gouverneur zare was not ze time. Of course it is imposseeble in Cancale to have ze grand bain of Paris, but then zare is still something, — a bath quite spécial, simple, and of ze people. Remember, monsieur, it is Bäader."

And so, with a cheery " Bon soir " from madame, and a profound bow from Bäader, I fell asleep.

The next morning I was awakened by a rumbling in the lower hold, as if the cargo was being shifted. Then came a noise like the moving of heavy barrels on the upper deck forward of the companionway. The next instant my door was burst open, and in stalked two brawny, big-armed fish-girls, yarn-stockinged to their knees, and with white sabots and caps. They were trundling the lower half of a huge hogshead.

"Pour le bain, monsieur," they both called out, bursting into laughter, as they rolled the mammoth tub behind my bed, grounded it with a revolving whirl, as a juggler would spin a plate, and disappeared, slamming the door behind them, their merriment growing fainter as they dropped down the companionway.

I peered over the head-board, and discovered the larger half of an enormous storage-barrel used for packing fish, with fresh saw-marks indenting its upper rim. Then I shouted for Bäader.

Before anybody answered, there came another onslaught, and in burst the same girls, carrying a great iron beach-kettle filled with water. This, with renewed fits of laughter, they dashed into the tub, and in a flash were off again, their wooden sabots clattering down the steps.

There was no mistaking the indication ; Bäader's bath had arrived.

I climbed up, and dropping in with both feet, avoiding the splinters and the nails, sat on the

sawed edge, ready for total immersion. Before
I could adjust myself to its conditions there
came another rush along the companionway,
accompanied by the same clatter of sabots and
splashing of water. There was no time to reach
the bed, and it was equally evident that I could
not vault out and throw myself against the door.
So I simply ducked down, held on, and shouted,
in French, Normandy patois, English : —

"Don't come in! Don't open the door!
Leave the water outside !" and the like. I
might as well have ruined my throat on a Cancale lugger driving before a gale. In burst the
door, and in swept the Amazons, letting go
another kettleful, this time over my upper half,
my lower half being squeezed down into the
tub.

When the girls had emptied the contents of
this last kettle over the edge, and caught sight
of my face, — they evidently thought I was still
behind the head-board, — both gave one prolonged shriek that literally roused the house.
The brawnier of the two, — a magnificent creature, with her corsets outside of her dress, —
after holding her sides with laughter until I
thought she would suffocate, sank upon the sea-
chest, from which her companion rescued her
just as Mme. Flamand and Bäader opened the

door. All this time my chin was resting on the jagged rim of the tub, and my teeth were chattering.

"Bäader, where in thunder have you been? Drag that chest against that door quick, and come in. Is this what you call a bath?"

"Monsieur, if you will pardon. I arouse myself at ze daylight; I rely upon Mme. Flamand that ze Englishman who is dead had left one behind; I search everywhere. Zen I make inquiry of ze mother of ze two demoiselles who have just gone. She was much insulted: she make ze bad face. She say with much indignation: 'Monsieur, since I was a baby ze water has not touched my body.' At ze supreme moment, when all hope was gone, I discover near ze house of ze same madame zis grand arrangement. Immediately I am on fire, and say to myself, 'Bäader, all is not lost. Even if zare was still ze bath of ze Englishman, it would not compare.' In ze quickness of an eye I bring a saw, and ze demoiselles are on zare knees making ze arrangement, one part big, one small. I say to myself, 'Bäader, monsieur is an artist, and of enthusiasm, and will appreciate zis utensile agréable of ze fisherman.' If monsieur will consider, it is, of course, not ze grand bain of Paris, but it is simple, and quite of ze people."

206

Some two months later, the governor and I happened to be strolling through the flower-market of the Madeleine. He had been selecting plants for the windows of his apartment, and needed a reliable man to arrange them in suitable boxes.

" That fellow Bäader lives down here somewhere ; perhaps he might know of some one," he said, consulting his notebook. " Yes ; No. 21 Rue Chambord. Let us look him up."

In five minutes we stood before a small, two-story house, with its door and wide basement-window protected by an awning. Beneath this, upon low shelves, was arranged a collection of wicker baskets, containing the several varieties of oysters from Normandy and Brittany coasts greatly beloved by Parisian epicures. On the top of each lid lay a tin sign bearing the name of the exact locality from which each toothsome bivalve was supposed to be shipped. These signs were all of one size.

The governor is a great lover of oysters, especially his own Chesapeakes, and his eye ran rapidly over the tempting exhibit as he read aloud, perhaps unconsciously to himself, the several labels : " Dinard, Paramé, Dieppe petite, Cancale spéciale." Then a new light seemed to break in upon him.

"Dieppe petite, Cancale spéciale," — here his face was a study, — "why, that's what Baader always called Cancale. By thunder! I believe that's where that fellow got his names. I don't believe the rascal was ever in Normandy in his life until I took him. Here, landlord!" A small shopkeeper, wearing an apron, ran out smiling, uncovering the baskets as he approached. "Do you happen to know a courier by the name of Bäader?"

"Never as courier, messieurs — always as commissionaire; he sells wood and charcoal to ze hotels. See! zare is his sign."

"Where does he live?"

"Upstairs."

"TINCTER OV IRON"

IT was in an old town in Connecticut. Marbles kept the shop. "Joseph Marbles, Shipwright and Blacksmith," the sign read.

I knew Joe. He had repaired one of the lighters used in carrying materials for the foundation of the lighthouse I was building. The town lay in the barren end of the State, where they raised rocks enough to make four stone fences to the acre. Joe always looked to me as if he had lived off the crop. The diet never affected his temper nor hardened his heart, so far as I could see. It was his body, his long, lean, lank body, that suggested the stone diet.

In his early days Joe had married a helpmate. She had lasted until the beginning of the third year, and then she had been carried to the cemetery on the hill, and another stone, and a new one, added to the general assortment. This matrimonial episode was his last.

This wife was a constant topic with Marbles. He would never speak of her as a part of his life, one who had shared his bed and board, and was therefore entitled to his love and reverent remembrance. It was rather as an appendage to his household, a curiosity, a natural freak, as one would discuss the habits of a chimpanzee, and with a certain pity, too, for the poor creature whom he had housed, fed, poked at, humored, and then buried.

And yet with it all I could always see that nothing else in his life had made so profound an impression upon him as the companionship of this "poor creeter," and that underneath his sparsely covered ribs there still glowed a spot for the woman who had given him her youth.

He would say, "It wuz one ov them days when she would n't eat," or "It was kind o' cur'us to watch her go on when she had one ov them tantrums." Sometimes he would recount some joke he had played upon her, rubbing his ribs in glee — holding his sides would have been a superfluous act and the statement here erroneous.

"That wuz when she fust come, yer know," he said to me one day, leaning against an old boat, his adze in his hand. "Her folks belonged over to Westerly. I never had seen much ov wimmen, and did n't know their ways. But I tell yer she wuz a queer 'un, allers imaginin'

she wuz ailin', er had heart disease when she
got out er breath runnin' upstairs, er as'mer,
er lumbago, er somethin' else dreadful. She
wuz the cur'usest critter, too, to take medicin'
ye ever see. She never ailed none really 'cept
when she broke her coller bone a-fallin' downstairs, and in the last sickness, the one that
killed her, but she believed all the time she
wuz, which wuz wuss. Every time the druggist would git out a new red card and stick it
in his winder, with a cure fer cold, er chilblains,
er croup, er e'sipelas, she 'd go and buy it, an'
out 'd cum ther cork, and she a-tastin' ov it
'fore she got hum. She used ter rub herself
with St. Jiminy's intment, and soak her feet
in sea-salt, and cover herself with plasters till
yer could n't rest. Why, ther cum a fellow
once who painted a yaller sign on ther whole
side ov Buckley's barn, — cure fer spiral men-
ingeetius, — and she wuz nigh crazy till she
had found out where ther pain ought ter be, and
had clapped er plaster on her back and front,
persuadin' herself she had it. That 's how she
bruk her coller bone, a-runnin' fer hot water to
soak 'em off, they burnt so, and stumblin'
over a kit ov tools I had brung hum to do a job
around the house. After this she begun ter run
down so, and git so thin and peaked, I begun to

think she really wuz goin' ter be sick, after all, jest fer a change.

" When ther doctor come, he sed it warn't nothin' but druggist's truck that ailed her, and he throwed what there wuz out er ther winder, and give her a tonic — Tincter ov Iron, he called it. Well, yer never see a woman hug a thing as she did that bottle. It was a spoonful three times a day, and then she 'd reach out fer it in ther night, vowin' it was doin' her a heap er good, and I a-gettin' ther bottle filled at Sarcy's ther druggist's, and payin' fifty cents every time he put er new cork in it. I tried ter reason with her, but it warn't no use ; she would have it, and if she could have got outer bed and looked round at the spring crop of advertisements on ther fences, she would hev struck somethin' worse. So I let her run on until she tuk about seven dollars' wuth of Tincter, and then dropped in ter Sarcy's. 'Sarcy,' sez I, ' can't ye wholesale this, er sell it by the quart ? If the ole woman's coller bone don't get ter runnin' easy purty soon, I 'll be broke.'

" ' Well,' he said, ' if I bought a dozen it might come cheaper, but it wuz a mighty pertic'ler medicine, and had ter be fixed just so.'

" ' 'T ain't pizen, is it ? ' I sez, ' thet 's got ter be fixed so all-fired kerful ? ' He 'lowed it warn't, and thet ye might take er barrel ov it and it would n't kill yer, but all ther same it has ter be made mighty pertic'ler.

"'Well, iron's cheap enough,' I sez, 'and strengthenin', too. If it's ther Tincter thet costs so, don't put so much in.' Well, he laffed, and said ther warn't no real iron in it, only Tincter, kinder iron soakage like, same es er drawin' ov tea.

"Goin' home thet night I got ter thinkin'. I'd been round iron all my life and knowed its ways, but I had n't struck no Tincter es I knowed ov. When she fell asleep I poured out a leetle in another bottle and slid it in my trousers pocket, an' next day, down ter ther shop, I tasted ov it and held it up ter ther light. It was kind er persimmony and dark-lookin', ez if it had rusty nails in it ; and so thet night when I goes hum I sez ter her, 'Down ter ther other druggist's I kin git twice as much Tincter fer fifty cents as I kin at Sarcy's, and if yer don't mind, I'll git it filled there.' Well, she never kicked a stroke, 'cept to say I'd better hurry, fer she had n't had a spoonful sence daylight, and she wuz beginnin' ter feel faint. When the whistle blew I cum hum ter dinner, and sot the new bottle, about twice as big as the other one, beside her bed.

213

" ' How 's that ? ' I sez. ' It 's a leetle grain darker and more muddy like, but the new druggist sez thet 's the Tincter, and thet 's what 's doin' ov yer good.' Well, she never suspicioned ; jest kept on, night and day, wrappin' herself round it every two er three hours, I gettin' it filled regerlar and she a-empt'in' ov it.

" 'Bout four weeks arter that she begun to git around, and then she 'd walk out ez fur ez ther shipyard fence, and then, begosh, she begun to flesh up so as you would n't know her. Now an' then she 'd meet the doctor, and she 'd say how she 'd never a-lived but fer ther Tincter, and he 'd laff and drive on. When she got real peart, I brought her down to the shop one day, and I shows her an old paint keg thet I kep' rusty bolts in, and half full ov water.

" ' Smell that,' I sez, and she smells it and cocks her eye.

" ' Taste it,' I sez, and she tasted it, and give me a look. Then I dips a spoonful out in a glass, and I sez : ' It 's most time to take yer medicine. I kin beat Gus Sarcy all holler makin' Tincter ; every drop yer drunk fer a month come out er thet keg.' "

"FIVE MEALS FOR A DOLLAR"

THE Literary Society of West Norrington, Vt., had invited me to lecture on a certain Tuesday night in February.

The Tuesday night had arrived. So had the train. So had the knock-kneed, bandy-legged hack, — two front wheels bowed in, two hind wheels bowed out, — and so had the lecturer.

West Norrington is built on a hill. At the foot are the station, a sawmill, and a glue factory. On the top is a flat plateau holding the principal residences, printing-office, opera-house, confectionery store, druggist's, and hotel. Up the incline is a scattering of cigar-stores, butcher-shops, real-estate agencies, and one lone restaurant. You know it is a restaurant by the pile of extra-dry oyster-shells in the window, — oysterless for months — and the four oranges bunched together in a wire basket like a nest of pool balls. You know it also from the sign, —

" Five meals for a dollar."

I saw this sign on my way up the hill, but

it made no impression on my mind. I was bound for the hotel — the West Norrington Arms, the conductor called it; and as I had eaten nothing since seven o'clock, and it was then four, I was absorbed mentally in arranging a bill of fare. Broiled chicken, of course, I said to myself, — always get delicious broiled chicken in the country, — and a salad, and perhaps — you can't always tell, of course, what the cellars of these old New England taverns may contain — yes, perhaps a pint of any really good Burgundy, Pommard, or Beaune.

"West Norrington Arms" sounded well. There was a distinct flavor of exclusiveness and comfort about it, suggesting old sideboards, hand-polished tables, small bar with cut-glass decanters, Franklin stoves in the bedrooms, and the like. I could already see the luncheon served in my room, the bright wood fire lighting up the dimity curtains draping the high-post bedstead. Yes, I would order Pommard.

Here the front knees came together with a jerk. Then the driver pulled his legs out of a buffalo robe, opened the door with a twist, and called out, —

"Nor'n't'n Arms."

I got out.

The first glance was not reassuring. It was

perhaps more Greek than Colonial or Early English or Late Dutch. Four high wooden boxes,
painted brown, were set up on end, — Doric col-
umns these, — supporting a pediment of like
material and color. Halfway up these supports
hung a balcony, where the Fourth of July ora-
tor always stands when he addresses his fellow
citizens. Old, of course, I said to myself —
early part of this century. Not exactly moss-
covered and inn-like, as I expected to find, but
inside it's all right.

"Please take in that bag and overcoat."
This to the driver, in a cheery tone.

The clerk was leaning over the counter, chewing a toothpick. Evidently he took me for a
drummer, for he stowed the bag behind the
desk, and hung the overcoat up on a nail in a
side room opening out of the office, and within
reach of his eye.

When I registered my name it made no per-
ceptible change in his manner. He said, "Want
supper?" with a tone in his voice that convinced me he had not heard a word of the Event
which brought me to West Norrington — I being
the Event.

"No, not now. I would like you to send to
my room in half an hour a broiled chicken, some
celery, and any vegetable which you can get

ready — and be good enough to put a pint of Burgundy " —

I did n't get any further. Something in his manner attracted me. I had not looked at him with any degree of interest before. He had been merely a medium for trunk check, room key, and ice water — nothing more.

Now I did. I saw a young man — a mean-looking young man — with a narrow, squeezed face, two flat glass eyes sewed in with red cotton, and a disastrous complexion. His hair was brushed like a barber's, with a scooping curl over the forehead ; his neck was long and thin, — so long that his apple looked over his collar's edge. This collar ran down to a white shirt decorated with a gold pin, the whole terminating in a low-cut velvet vest.

" Supper at seven," he said.

This, too, came with a jerk.

" Yes, I know, but I have n't eaten anything since breakfast, and don't want to wait until " —

" Ain't nuthin' cooked 'tween meals. Supper at seven."

" Can't I get " —

" Yer can't get nuthin' until supper-time, and yer won't get no Burgundy then. Yer could n't get a bottle in Norrington with a club. This town's prohibition. Want a room?" This last word was almost shouted in my ear.

"Yes — one with a wood fire." I kept my temper.

"Front!" — this to a boy half asleep on a bench. "Take this bag to No. 37, and turn on the steam. Your turn next," — and he handed the pen to a fresh arrival, who had walked up from the train.

No. 37 contained a full set of Michigan furniture, including a patent wash-stand that folded up to look like a bookcase, smelt slightly of varnish, and was as hot as a Pullman sleeper.

I threw up all the windows ; came down and tackled the clerk again.

" Is there a restaurant near by ? "

" Next block above. Nichols."

He never looked up — just kept on chewing the toothpick.

" Is there another hotel here ? "

Even a worm will turn.

" No."

That settled it. I did n't know any inhabitant — not even a committeeman. It was the West Norrington Arms or the street.

So I started for Nichols'. By that time I could have eaten the shingles off the church.

Nichols' proved to be a one-and-a-half-story

house with a glass door, a calico curtain, and a jingle bell. Inside was a cake shop, presided over by a thin woman in a gingham dress and black lace cap and wig. In the rear stood a marble-top table with iron legs. This made it a restaurant.

"Can you get me something to eat ? Steak, ham and eggs — anything ?" I had fallen in my desires.

She looked me all over. "Well, I 'm 'mazin' sorry, but I guess you 'll have to excuse us; we 're just bakin', and this is our busy day. S'mother time we should like to, but to-day " —

I closed the door and was in the street again. I had no time for lengthy discussions that did n't lead to something tangible and eatable.

"Alone in London," I said to myself. "Lost in New York. Adrift in West Norrington. Plenty of money to buy, and nobody to sell. Everybody going about their business with full stomachs, happy, contented, — all with homes, and firesides, and ice chests, and things hanging to cellar rafters, hams and such like, and I a wanderer and hungry, an outcast, a tramp."

Then I thought some citizen might take me in. She was a rather amiable-looking old lady, with a kind, motherly face.

"Madam !" This time I took off my hat. Ah,

the common law of hunger brings you down and humbles your pride. "Do you live here, madam ?"

"Why, yes, sir," edging to the sidewalk.

"Madam, I am a stranger here, and very hungry. It's baking-day at Nichols'. Do you know where I can get anything to eat ?"

"Well, no, I can't rightly say," still eyeing me suspiciously. "Hungry, be ye ? Well, that's too bad, and Nichols baking."

I corroborated all these statements, standing bareheaded, a wild idea running through my head that her heart would soften and she would take me home and set me down in a big chintz-covered rocking-chair, near the geraniums in the windows, and have her daughter — a nice, fresh, rosy-cheeked girl in an apron — go out into the buttery and bring in white cheese, and big slices of bread, and some milk, and preserves, and a — But the picture was never completed.

"Well," she said slowly, " if Nichols is baking, I guess ye 'll hev to wait till supper-time."

Then like a sail to a drowning man there rose before me the sign down the hill near the station, "Five meals for a dollar."

I had the money. I had the appetite. I would eat them all at once, and *now.*

In five minutes I was abreast of the extra-dry oyster-shells and the pool balls. Then I pushed open the door.

Inside there was a long room, bare of everything but a wooden counter, upon which stood a glass case filled with cigars ; behind this was a row of shelves with jars of candy, and level with the lower shelf my eye caught a slouch hat. The hat covered the head of the proprietor. He was sitting on a stool, sorting out chewing-gum.

"Can I get something to eat ?"

The hat rose until it stood six feet in the air, surmounting a round, good-natured face, ending in a chin whisker.

"Cert. What 'll yer hev ?"

Here at last was peace and comfort and food and things ! I could hardly restrain myself.

"Anything. Steak, fried potatoes — what have you got ?"

"Waal, I dunno. 'T ain't time yit for supper, but we kin fix ye somehow. Lemme see."

Then he pushed back a curtain that screened one half of the room, disclosing three square tables with white cloths and casters, and disappeared through a rear door.

"We got a steak," he said, dividing the curtains again, "but the potatoes is out."

222

"Any celery ?"

"No. Guess can git ye some 'cross to ther grocery. Won't take a minit."

"All right. Could you" —and I lowered my voice — "could you get me a bottle of beer ?"

"Yes — if you got a doctor's prescription."

"Could *you* write one ?" I asked nervously.

"I 'll try." And he laughed.

In two minutes he was back, carrying four bunches of celery and a paper box marked "Paraffine candles."

"What preserves have you ?"

"Waal, any kind."

"Raspberry jam, or apricots ?" I inquired, my spirits rising.

"We ain't got no rusberry, but we got peaches."

"Anything else ?"

"Waal, no ; come ter look 'em over, just peaches."

So he added a can to the celery and candles, and carried the whole to the rear.

While he was gone I leaned over the cigar-case and examined the stock. One box labelled "Bouquet" attracted my eye ; each cigar had a little paper band around its middle. I remembered the name, and determined to smoke one after dinner if it took my last cent.

Then a third person took a hand in the feast. This was the hired girl, who came in with a tray. She wore an alpaca dress and a disgusted expression. It was evident that she resented my hunger as a personal affront — stopping everything to get supper two hours ahead of time ! She did n't say this aloud, but I knew it all the same.

Then more tray, with a covered dish the size of a soap-cup, a few sprigs of celery out of the four bunches, and a preserve dish about the size of a butter pat, containing four pieces of peach swimming in their own juice.

In the soap-dish lay the steak. It was four inches in diameter and a quarter of an inch thick. I opened the paraffine candles, poured out half a glass, and demolished the celery and peaches. I did n't want to muss up the steak. I was afraid I might bend it, and spoil it for some one else.

Then an idea struck me : " Could she poach me some eggs ?"

She supposed she could, if she could find the eggs ; most everything was locked up this time of day.

I waited, and spread the mustard on the dry bread, and had more peaches and paraffine. When the eggs came they excited my sympathies. They were such innocent-looking things — pinched and shrivelled up, as if they had fainted at sight of the hot water and died in great agony. The toast, too, on which they were coffined, had a cremated look. Even the hired girl saw this. She said it was a "leetle mite too much browned; she 'd forgot it watchin' the eggs."

Here the street door opened, and a young woman entered and asked for two papers of chewing-gum.

She got them, but not until the proprietor had shot together the curtains screening off the candy store from the restaurant. The dignity and exclusiveness of the establishment required this.

When she was gone, I poured out the rest of the paraffine, and called out through the closed curtains for a cigar.

" One of them bo-kets ?" came the proprietor's voice in response.

" Yes, one of them."

He brought it himself, in his hand, just as it was, holding the mouth end between the thumb and forefinger.

" And now how much ?"

He made a rapid accounting, overlooking the table, his eyes lighting on the several fragments:

225

"Beer, ten cents ; steak, ten ; peaches, five ; celery, three ; eggs on toast, ten ; one bo-ket, four." Then he paused a moment, as if he wanted to be entirely fair and square, and said, "Forty-two cents."

When I reached the hotel, a man who said he was the proprietor came to my room. He was a sad man, with tears in his voice.

"You 're comin' to supper, ain't ye ? It 'll be the last time. It 's a kind o' mournful occasion, but I like to have ye."

It was now my turn.

"No, I 'm not coming to supper. You drove me out of here half starving into the street two hours ago. I could n't get anything to eat at Nichols', and so I had to go down the hill to a place near the sawmill, where I got the most infernal " —

He stopped me with a look of real anxiety.

"Not the five-meals-for-a-dollar place ?"

"Yes."

"And you swallowed it ?"

"Certainly — poached eggs, peaches, and a lot of things."

"No," he said reflectively, looking at me curiously. "*You* don't want no supper — prob-'bility is you won't want no breakfast either. You 'd better eaten the sawmill — it would 'er set lighter. If I 'd known who you were, I 'd tried " —

" But I told the clerk," I broke in.

" What clerk ?" he interrupted in an astonished tone.

" Why, the clerk at the desk, where I registered, — that long-necked crane with red eyes."

" He ain't no clerk ; we ain't had one for a week. Don't you know what 's goin' on ? Ain't you read the bills ? Step out into the hall — there 's one posted up right in front of you. ' Sheriff's sale ; all the stock and fixtures of the Norrington Arms to be sold on Wednesday morning ' — that 's to-morrow — ' by order of the Court.' You can read the rest yourself ; print 's too fine for me. That fellow you call a crane is a deputy sheriff. He 's takin' charge, while we eat up what 's in the house."

"NEVER HAD NO SLEEP"

IT was on the upper deck of a Chesapeake
Bay boat en route for Old Point Comfort
and Norfolk. I was bound for Norfolk.

"Kinder ca'm, ain't it?"

The voice proceeded from a pinched-up old
fellow with a colorless face, straggling white
beard, and sharp eyes. He wore a flat-topped
slouch hat resting on his ears, and a red silk
handkerchief tied in a sporting knot around his
neck. His teeth were missing, the lips puckered
up like the mouth of a sponge-bag. In his
hand he carried a cane with a round ivory
handle. This served as a prop to his mouth,
the puckered lips fumbling about the knob.
He was shadowed by an old woman wearing
a shiny brown silk, that glistened like a wet
waterproof, black mitts, poke-bonnet, flat lace
collar, and a long gold watch chain. I had noticed them at supper. She was cutting up his
food.

"Kinder ca'm, ain't it?" he exclaimed again,
looking my way. "Fust real nat'ral vittles I 've

228

eat fur a year. 'Spect it's ther sea air. This water's brackish, ain't it?"

I confirmed his diagnosis of the saline qualities of the Chesapeake, and asked if he had been an invalid.

"Waal, I should say so! Bin livin' on hospital mush fur nigh on ter a year; but, by gum! ter-night I jist said ter Mommie: 'Mommie, shuv them soft-shells this way. Ain't seen none sence I kep' tavern.' "

Mommie nodded her head in confirmation, but with an air of "if you're dead in the morning, don't blame me."

"What's been the trouble?" I inquired, drawing up a camp stool.

"Waal, I dunno rightly. Got my stummic out o' gear, throat kinder weak, and what with the seventies" —

"Seventies?" I asked.

"Yes; hed 'em four year. I'm seventy-five nex' buthday. But come ter sum it all up, what's ther matter with me is I ain't never hed no sleep. Let me sit on t'other side. One ear's stopped workin' this ten year."

He moved across and pulled an old cloak around him.

"Been long without sleep?" I asked sympathetically.

229

" 'Bout sixty year — mebbe sixty-five."

I looked at him inquiringly, fearing to break the thread if I jarred too heavily.

"Yes, 'spect it must be more. Well, you keep tally. Five year bootblack and porter in a tavern in Dover, 'leven year tendin' bar down in Wilmington, fourteen year bootcherin', nineteen year an' six months keepin' a roadhouse ten miles from Philadelphy fur ther hucksters comin' to market — quit las' summer. How much yer got ? "

I nodded, assenting to his estimate of sixty-five years of service, if he had started when fifteen.

He ruminated for a time, caressing the ivory ball of his cane with his uncertain mouth.

I jogged him again. " Boots and tending bar I should think would be wakeful, but I did n't suppose butchering and keeping hotel necessitated late hours."

"Well, — that 's 'cause yer don't know. Bootcherin 's ther wakefullest business as is. Now yer a country bootcher, mind — no city beef man, nor porterhouse steak and lamb chops fur clubs an' hotels, but jest an all-round bootcher — lamb, veal, beef, mebbe once a week, ha'f er whole, as yer trade goes. Now ye kill when ther sun goes down, so ther flies

230

can't mummuck 'em. Next yer head and leg
'em, gittin' in in rough, as we call it—takin'
out ther insides an' leavin' ther hide on ther
back. Ye let 'em hang fur four hours, and 'bout
midnight ye go at 'em agin, trim an' quarter,
an' 'bout four in winter and three in summer
ye open up ther stable with a lantern, git yer
stuff in, an' begin yer rounds."

"Yes, I see ; but keeping hotel is n't"—

"Now thar ye're dead out agin. Ye're
a-keepin' a roadhouse, mind,—one of them
huckster taverns where ha'f yer folks come in
'arly 'bout sundown and sit up ha'f ther night,
and t'other ha'f drive inter yer yard 'bout midnight an' lie 'round till daybreak. It's eat er
drink all ther time, and by ther time ye've
stood behind ther bar and jerked down ev'ry
bottle on ther shelf, gone out ha'f a dozen
times with er light ter keep some mule from
kickin' out yer partitions, got er dozen winks
on er settee in a back room, and then begin
bawlin' upstairs, routin' out two or three hired
gals to get 'arly breakfust, ye're nigh tuckered
out. By ther time this gang is fed, here comes
another drivin' in. Oh, thet's a nice quiet life,
thet is ! I quit las' year, and me and Mommie
is on our way to Old P'int Cumfut. I ain't
never bin thar, but ther name sounded peaceful

231

like, and so I tho't ter try it. I 'm in sarch er
sleep, I am. Wust thing 'bout me is, no matter whar I 'm lyin', when it comes three 'clock
I 'm out of bed. Bin at it all my life; can't
never break it."

"But you 've enjoyed life?" I interpo-
lated.

"Enj'yed life? Well, p'rhaps, and agin
p'rhaps not," looking furtively at his wife.
Then, lowering his voice: "There ain't bin er
horse race within er hundred miles of Philadelphy I ain't tuk in. Enj'y! Well, don't yer
worry." And his sharp eyes snapped.

I believed him. That accounted for the way
the red handkerchief was tied loosely round his
throat, — an old road-wagon trick to keep the
dust out.

For some minutes he nursed his knees with
his hands, rocking himself to and fro, smiling
gleefully, thinking, no doubt, of the days he
had speeded down the turnpike, and the seats,
too, on the grand stand.

I jogged him again, venturing the remark that
I should think that now he might try and cor-
ral a nap in the daytime.

The gleeful expression faded instantly. "See
here," he said seriously, laying his hand with
a warning gesture on my arm, the ivory knob

popping out of the sponge-bag. "Don't yer never take no sleep in ther daytime; that's suicide. An' if yer sleep after eatin', that's murder. Look at me. Kinder peaked, ain't I? Stummic gone, throat busted, mouth caved in; but I'm seventy-five, ain't I? An' I ain't a wreck yet, am I? An' a-goin' to Old P'int Cumfut, ain't we, me an' Mommie, who's sixty — Never mind, Mommie. I won't give it away" — with a sly wink at me. The old woman looked relieved. "Now jist s'pose I'd sat all my life on my back stoop, ha'f awake, an' ev'ry time I eat, lie down an' go ter sleep. Waal, yer'd never bin talkin' to-night to old Jeb Walters. They'd 'a' bin fertilizin' gardin truck with him. I've seen more 'n a dozen of my friends die thet way — busted on this back porch snoozin' business. Fust they git loggy 'bout ther gills; then their knees begin ter swell; purty soon they're hobblin' round on er cane; an' fust thing they know they're tucked away in er number thirteen coffin, an' ther daisies a-bloomin' over 'em. None er that fur me. Come, Mommie, we'll turn in."

When the boat, next morning, touched the pier at Old Point, I met the old fellow and his wife waiting for the plank to be hauled aboard.

"Did you sleep?" I asked.

233

"Sleep? Waal, I could, p'rhaps, if I knowed ther ways aboard this steamboat. There come er nigger to my room 'bout midnight, and wanted ter know if I was ther gentleman that had lost his carpet-bag — he had it with him. Waal, of course I warn't; and then 'bout three, jist as I tho't I was dozin' off agin, ther come ther dangdest poundin' the nex' room ter mine ye ever heard. Mommie, she said 't was fire, but I did n't smell no smoke. Wrong room agin. Feller nex' door was to go ashore in a scow with some dogs and guns. They 'd a-slowed down and was waitin', an' they could n't wake him up. Mebbe I 'll git some sleep down ter Old P'int Cumfut, but I ain't 'spectin' nuthin'. By, by."

And he disappeared down the gangplank.

MY NEW LANGUAGE

SOME years ago I determined on a sketching tour through Spain and Portugal. I
wanted old church walls fringed with pomegran-
ates, strings of mules laden with skins of wine,
señoritas with red-heeled slippers, and the like.

Sam, my travelling companion, said he did
n't know a word of the language, and I knew
that we could n't do anything without it ;
better stay at home. Sam is not my servant,
remember, but my chum. He 's not an artist,
but a " buggist " with a leaning toward butter-
flies. He 's got another name — two of them —
the last with three syllables, but it is unneces-
sary to mention them here. And then again,
Sam would n't like it. So I sent for old Morales
— Professor Ceballos Morales, teacher of modern languages — Italian, German, French, and
Spanish. I speak the first three like a native
— of New York.

When Morales presented himself, he proved
to be a sun-dried Hidalgo, with a wrinkled, sad-
dle-colored skin, a broken assortment of teeth,

— three gone, — a sharp nose, two quick, restless eyes, a brown wig, and a pair of pointed mustachios.

The Professor bowed as low as Sancho would have done to Don Quixote, rested his hooked cane against my easel, laid his hat on the floor, drew off a pair of green kid gloves, and said that in "four week — seex at te mostest" — he could teach me "te langwidge." Not, of course, to "hablar" with "perfectione," but so that I could travel through the land of his birth with ease and safety.

So we started in.

It was June, cool, lovely, leafy June, everywhere except under the glass of my skylight. There it was as hot as the hinges of Hades. But I kept at it. I had verbs with my coffee, nouns with my luncheon, and short sentences with my dinner. Wherever I went I carried a grammar in my outside pocket. This I studied on street corners during the day and under the gaslights at night while waiting for trolleys and horse-cars.

By the end of the second week I could ask for the green umbrella of my grandfather and the new hat of my aunt. By the end of the fourth week the Professor could say to me, "It is not the bird that flies but the camel that walks," and I understood him ! — got the camel right every time.

This knowledge brought a rapture with it to which, up to that moment, I had been a stranger.

By the end of the sixth week — the week I sailed — I was discharged cured. Even the Professor admitted it, and would stand on the stairs outside my studio door and wave me adios and wish me buenos dias with the same shrug of his shoulders and upward chicken-drinking glance of the eye that he would have given any other caballero of his acquaintance.

Under the quickening impulse of these last subtle touches, I began to be on good terms with myself. No señorita would turn away from me now with a blank stare ; no hotel-keeper would fleece me out of my last peseta ; no bull-fighter would pass me by unnoticed. A twist to my mustache, a dash of garlic in my salad, and one word of this pure unadulterated Castilian accent which I had just acquired, and I would be recognized as one of them.

But my greatest triumph would be over Sam. Sam knew German, French, and some English — not much that was pure, but enough. He could get a wiener-schnitzel in any café in Munich, and could ask his way back to his hotel across the Seine without having to go round by the Arc de Triomphe, but he would be stranded and dead broke when it came to pure Castilian. The certainty, therefore, of his being dependent on me for his bare meat and shelter while in sunny Spain was to be the supremest part of the joy of his companionship.

On the way across the ocean I thumbed the grammar every hour of the day and held private lessons with myself, conjugating verbs and arranging conversations with imaginary hotel-keepers and travellers. I was afraid I would lose my grip on what I had if I slackened my hold a single hour. Sam said in his choicest English "that if I didn't stop workin' my mouth that way, a-chewin' Spanish, they'd take me for a missionary mumblin' aves for my sins." I quote this to show some of the things I have to put up with in Sam.

When we landed, took train, and stopped at Hendaye, — the last station in France, — I became more bold. I told Sam — not offensively, but with a sense of the importance of the announcement — that hereafter I should confine myself entirely to the language of the country. This, I added, was a courtesy I owed the inhabitants.

In proof of this resolution, I began on the first

native I met — a kiln-dried caballero this time
— seated opposite me in the compartment. He
was years younger than the Professor, and had
a cigarette glued to his lower lip, which wab-
bled as he talked, but never lost its hold. He
listened attentively and courteously for the first
half hour, answering me in such monosyllables
as "Cierto," "Bueno," "Es verdad," etc., —
even Sam understood these — and then, whispered to Sam in French, so this beast of a chum
told me afterwards : "Does the amiable Hidalgo speak any other language but Spanish ? "

I saw Sam double up, cram his pudgy fist
into his mouth and catch his breath, but we
were nearing the frontier, and I was too intent
on framing my first sentence on Spanish soil to
give him any attention. The first thing needed
was a porter, as our traps must be taken from
the train and carried to the Custom House. So
I ran my finger down the P's of my dictionary,
found the word, and instantly constructed the
sentence.

"Cargador (porter), deseo (I wish) un
hombre (a man) tomar (to take) mis cosas
(my things)."

Then I fired it point-blank at a fellow in a
blue blouse.

On the blouse's second trip I blazed away

239

again, modulating the accent this time, beginning " Cargador " in a careless, even slightly familiar way, as if I were resuming a conversation in which I had forgotten to mention my small baggage then on the platform before me where the trainman had dumped it. No response — not even a side glance.

Sam winked at the caballero with the cigarette — everybody had to get out at the frontier — and passed his hand over his face. I turned my back, opened my phrase-book, went over all the words, satisfied myself that they were not only correct Spanish but elegant Castilian, waited for the third trip of the blouse, and roared out in his ear : —

" Cargador, deseo un hombre tomar mis cosas."

The man stopped, tilted his truck, pushed his cap back from his forehead, and said, in a rich North of Ireland brogue : " I hear yez ; if ye 'll howld that clack o' yours, I 'll sind a man ter take yer thraps."

When Sam got through laughing, I walked to the edge of the platform, took the dictionary and phrase-book from my inside pocket, and with the supremest satisfaction dropped them into the ditch.

THE MAN FROM TROY

HE was backed up against the Column of the Lion, holding at bay a horde of gondoliers, who were shrieking, "Gondola! Gondola!" as only Venetian gondoliers can. He had a half-defiant look, like a cornered stag, as he stood there protecting a small wizen-faced woman of an uncertain age, dressed in a long gray silk duster and pigeon-winged hat, — one of those hats that looked as if the pigeon had alighted on it and exploded.

"No, durn ye, I don't want no gon-*do*-la; I got one somewhere round here if I can find it."

If his tall gaunt frame, black chin whisker, and clearly defined features had not located him instantly in my mind, his dialect would have done so.

"You 'll probably find your gondola at the next landing," I said, pointing to the steps.

He looked at me kindly, took the woman by the arm, as if she had been under arrest, and marched her to the spot indicated.

In another moment I felt a touch on my shoulder. " Neighbor, ain't you from the U. S. A. ? "

I nodded my head.

"Shake ! It's God's own land ! " and he disappeared in the throng.

The next morning I was taking my coffee in the café at the Britannia, when I caught a pair of black eyes peering over a cup, at a table opposite. Then six feet and an inch or two of raw untilled American rose in the air, picked up his plates, cup, and saucer, and, crossing the room, hooked out a chair with his left foot from my table, and sat down.

" You 're the painter feller that helped me out of a hole yesterday ? Yes, I knowed it ; I see you come in to dinner last night. Elizabeth said it was you, but you was so almighty rigged up in that swallow-tailed coat of yourn I did n't catch on for a minute, but Eliza-beth said she was dead sure."

" The lady with you — your wife ? "

" Not to any alarming extent, young man. Never had one — she 's my sister — only one I got ; and this summer she took it into her head — you don't mind my setting here, do you ? I 'm so durned lonesome among these jabbering Greeks I 'm nearly froze stiff. Thank

ye ! — took it into her head she'd come over
here, and of course I had to bring her. You
ain't never travelled around, perhaps, with a
young girl of fifty-five, with her head crammed
full of hifalutin' notions, — convents and early
masters and Mont Blancs and Bon Marchés, —
with just enough French to make a muddle of
everything she wants to get. Up before daylight
to see the place where Mary Antoinette was
hung and Bonyparte was buried. Climbin' up
every old pair of stairs she can poke her nose
into till her legs ache so she can't rest nights.
Well, that's Eliza-beth. First it was a circu-
lating library, at Unionville, back of Troy,
where I live ; then come a course of lectures
twice a week on old Edinburgh and the Alps and
German cities ; and then, to cap all, there come
a cuss with magic-lantern slides of 'most every
old ruin in Europe, and half our women were
crazy to get away from home, and Eliza-beth
worse than any of 'em ; and so I got a couple
of Cook's tickets out and back, and here we are ;
and I don't mind saying," and a wicked, vin-
dictive look filled his eyes, "that of all the
cussed holes I ever got into in my life, this here
Venice takes — the — cake. Here, John Henry,
bring me another cup of coffee ; this's stone-
cold. P. D. Q. now ! Don't let me have to

build a fire under you." This to a waiter speaking every language but English.

"Do not the palaces interest you?" I asked inquiringly, in my effort to broaden his views.

"Palaces be durned! Excuse my French. Palaces! A lot of caved-in old rookeries; with everybody living on the second floor because the first one 's so damp ye 'd get your die-and-never-get-over-it if you lived in the basement, and the top floors so leaky that you go to bed under an umbrella; and they all braced up with iron clamps to keep 'em from falling into the canal, and not a square inch on any one of 'em clean enough to dry a shirt on! What kind of holes are they for decent— Now see here," laying his hand confidingly on my shoulder, "just answer me one question— you seem like a level-headed young man, and ought to give it to me straight. Been here all summer, ain't you?"

"Yes."

"Been comin' years, ain't you?"

I nodded my head.

"Well, now, I want it straight," — and he lowered his voice, — "what does a sensible man find in an old waterlogged town like this?"

I gave him the customary answer: the glories of her past; the picturesque life of the lagoons; the beauty of her palaces, churches, and gardens; the luxurious gondolas, etc., etc.

"Don't see it," he broke out before I had half finished. "As for the gon-do-las, you're dead right, and no mistake. First time I settled on one of them cushions I felt just as if I'd settled in a basket of kittens; but as for palaces! Why, the State House at Al-ba-ny knocks 'em cold; and as for gardens! Lord! when I think of mine at home all chock-full of hollyhocks and sunflowers and morning-glories, and then think what a first-class cast-iron idiot I am wandering around here" — He gazed abstractedly at the ceiling for a moment as if the thought overpowered him, and then went on, "I've got a stock-farm six miles from Unionville, where I've got some three-year-olds can trot in 2.23 — Gardens!" — suddenly remembering his first train of thought, — "they simply ain't in it. And as for ler-goons! We've got a river sailing along in front of Troy that may n't be so wide, but it's a durned sight safer and longer, and there ain't a gallon of water in it that ain't as sweet as a daisy; and that's what you can't say of these streaks of mud around here, that smell like a dumping-ground." Here he rose from his chair, his voice filling the room, the words dropping slowly: "I — ain't — got — no — use —

245

for — a — place — where — there — ain't — a
— horse — in — the — town, — and — every —
cellar — is — half — full — of — water."

A few mornings after, I was stepping into
my gondola when I caught sight of the man
from Troy sitting in a gondola surrounded by
his trunks. His face expressed supreme con-
tent, illumined by a sort of grim humor, as if
some master effort of his life had been rewarded
with more than usual success. Eliza-beth was
tucked away on "the basket of kittens," half
hidden by the linen curtains.

"Off ? " I said inquiringly.

"You bet ! "

"Which way ? "

"Paris, and then a bee-line for New York."

"But you are an hour too early for your
train."

He held his finger to his lips and knitted his
eyebrows.

"What 's that ? " came a shrill plaintive
voice from the curtains. "An hour more ?
George, please ask the gentleman to tell the
gondolier to take us to Salviate's ; we 've got
time for that glass mirror, and I can't bear to
leave Venice without " —

"Eliza-beth, you sit where you air, if it takes
a week. No Salviate's in mine, and no glass

246

mirror. We are stuffed now so jammed full of wooden goats, glass bottles, copper buckets, and old church rags that I had to jump on my trunk to lock it." Then waving his hand to me, he called out as I floated off, " This craft is pointed for home, and don't you forget it."

THE BOY IN THE CLOTH CAP

I HAD seen the little fellow but a moment before, standing on the car platform and peering wistfully into the night, as if seeking some face in the hurrying crowd at the station. I remembered distinctly the cloth cap pulled down over his ears, his chubby, rosy cheeks, and the small baby hand clutching the iron rail of the car, as I pushed by and sprang into a hack.

"Lively, now, cabby ; I have n't a minute," and I handed my driver a trunk check.

Outside the snow whirled and eddied, the drifts glistening white in the glare of the electric light.

I drew my fur coat closer around my throat, and beat an impatient tattoo with my feet. The storm had delayed the train, and I had less than an hour in which to dine, dress, and reach my audience.

Two minutes later something struck the cab with a force that rattled every spoke in the wheels. It was my trunk, and cabby's head, white with snow, was thrust through the window.

"Morgan House, did you say, boss ? "

" Yes, and on the double-quick."

Another voice now sifted in, — a small, thin, pleading voice, too low and indistinct for me to catch the words from where I sat.

" Want to go where ? " cried cabby. The conversation was like one over the telephone, in which only one side is heard. " To the orphan asylum ? Why, that 's three miles from here. . . . Walk ? . . . See here, sonny, you would n't get halfway. . . . No, I can't take yer — got a load."

My own head had filled the window now.

"Here, cabby, don't stand there all night ! What 's the matter, anyway ? "

" It 's a boy, boss, about a foot high, wants to walk to the orphan 'sylum."

" Pass him in."

He did, literally, through the window, without opening the door, his little wet shoes first, then his sturdy legs in wool stockings, round body encased in a pea-jacket, and last, his head, covered by the same cloth cap I had seen on the platform. I caught him, feet first, and helped land him on the front seat, where he sat looking at me with staring eyes that shone all the brighter in the glare of the arc light. Next a collar-box and a small paper bundle were handed in. These the little fellow clutched eagerly, one in each hand, his eyes still looking into mine.

"Are you an orphan?" I asked, — a wholly thoughtless question, of course.

"Yes, sir."

"Got no father nor mother?"

Another, equally idiotic; but my interest in the boy had been inspired by the idea of the saving of valuable minutes. As long as he stood outside in the snow, he was an obstruction. Once aboard, I could take my time in solving his difficulties.

"Got a father, sir, but my mother's dead."

We were now whirling up the street, the cab lighting up and growing pitch dark by turns, depending on the location of the street lamps.

"Where's your father?"

"Went away, sir." He spoke the words without the slightest change in his voice, neither abashed nor too bold, but with a simple straightforwardness which convinced me of their truth.

"Do you want to go to the asylum?"

"Yes, sir."

"Why?"

" Because I can learn everything there is to learn, and there is n't any other place for me to go."

This was said with equal simplicity. No whining; no " me mother 's dead, sir, an' I ain't had nothin' to eat all day," etc. Not that air about him at all. It was merely the statement of a fact which he felt sure I knew all about.

" What 's your name ? "

" Ned."

" Ned what ? "

" Ned Rankin, sir."

" How old are you ? "

" I 'm eight " — then thoughtfully — " no, I 'm nine years old."

" Where do you live ? "

I was firing these questions one after the other without the slightest interest in either the boy or his welfare. My mind was on my lecture, and the impatient look on the faces of the audience, and the consulted watch of the chairman of the committee, followed by the inevitable : " You are not very prompt, sir," etc. " Our people have been in their seats," etc. If the boy had previously replied to my question as to where he lived, I had forgotten the name of the town.

"I live" — Then he stopped. "I live in —
Do you mean now?" he added simply.

"Yes."

There was another pause. "I don't know,
sir; maybe they won't let me stay."

Another foolish question. Of course, if he
had left home for good, and was now on his
way to the asylum for the first time, his present
home was this hack.

But he had won my interest now. His words
had come in tones of such directness, and were
so calm, and gave so full a statement of the
exact facts, that I leaned over quickly, and
began studying him a little closer.

I saw that this scrap of a boy wore a gray
woollen suit, and I noticed that the cap was
made of the same cloth as the jacket, and that
both were the work of some inexperienced hand,
with uneven, unpressed seams, — the seams of
a flatiron, not a tailor's goose. Instinctively
my mind went back to what his earlier life had
been.

"Have you got any brothers and sisters, my
boy?"

"Yes, sir."

"Where are they?"

"I don't know, sir; I was too little to remember."

The pathos of this answer stirred me all the more.

"Who 's been taking care of you ever since your father left you? " I had lowered my voice now to a more confidential tone.

" A German man."

"What did you leave him for? "

" He had no work, and he took me to the priest."

" When? "

" Last week, sir."

"What did the priest do? "

" He gave me these clothes. Don't you think they 're nice? The priest's sister made them for me — all but the stockings; she bought those."

As he said this, he lifted his arms so I could look under them, and thrust out toward me his two plump legs. I said the clothes were very nice, and that I thought they fitted him very well, and I felt his chubby knees and calves as I spoke, and ended by getting hold of his soft wee hand, which I held on to. His fingers closed tightly over mine, and a slight smile lighted up his face. It seemed good to him to have something to hold on to. I began again, —

" Did the priest send you here? "

"Yes, sir. Do you want to see the letter? "

253

The little hand — the free one — fumbled under the jacket, loosened the two lower buttons, and disclosed a white envelope pinned to his shirt.

"I'm to give it to 'em at the asylum. But I can't unpin it. He told me not to."

"That's right, my boy. Leave it where it is."

"You poor little rat," I said to myself. "This is pretty rough on you. You ought to be tucked up in some warm bed, not out here alone in this storm."

The boy felt for the pin in the letter, reassured himself that it was safe, and carefully rebuttoned his jacket. I looked out of the window, and caught glimpses of houses flying by, with lights in their windows, and now and then the cheery blaze of a fire. Then I looked into his eyes again. I still had hold of his hand.

"Surely," I said to myself, "this boy must have some one soul who cares for him." I determined to go a little deeper.

"How did you get here, my boy?" I had leaned nearer to him.

"The priest put me on the train, and a lady told me where to get off."

"Oh, a lady!" Now I was getting at it! Then he was not so desolate; a lady had looked

after him. " What 's her name ? " This with
increased eagerness.

" She did n't tell me, sir."

I sank back on my seat. No ! I was all wrong.
It was a positive, undeniable, piteous fact. Sev-
enty millions of people about him, and not one
living soul to look to ! Not a tie that connected
him with anything. A leaf blown across a field;
a bottle adrift in the sea, sailing from no port and
bound for no haven. I got hold of his other
hand, and looked down into his eyes, and an
almost irresistible desire seized me to pick him
up in my arms and hug him ; he was too big
to kiss, and too little to shake hands with ;
hugging was all there was left. But I did n't.
There was something in his face that repelled
any such familiarity, — a quiet dignity, pluck,
and patience that inspired more respect than
tenderness, that would make one want rather
to touch his hat to him.

Here the cab stopped with so sudden a jerk
that I had to catch him by the arms to steady
him. Cabby opened the door.

" Morgan House, boss. Goin' 's awful, or I'd
got ye here sooner."

The boy looked up into my face ; not with
any show of uneasiness, only a calm patience.
If he was to walk now, he was ready.

255

" Cabby, how far is it to the asylum ? " I asked.

" 'Bout a mile and a half."

"Throw that trunk off and drive on. This boy can't walk."

" I 'll take him, boss."

" No ; I 'll take him myself. Lively, now."

I looked at my watch. Twenty minutes of the hour had gone. I would still have time to jump into a dress suit, but the dinner must be brief. There came a seesaw rocking, then a rebound, and a heavy thud told where the trunk had fallen. The cab sped on round a sharp corner, through a narrow street, and across a wide square.

Suddenly a thought rushed over me that culminated in a creeping chill. Where was his trunk ? In my anxiety over my own, I had forgotten the boy's.

I turned quickly to the window, and shouted,

" Cabby ! *Cabby* , you did n't leave the boy's trunk, too, did you ? "

The little fellow slid down from the seat, and began fumbling around in the dark.

" No, sir; I 've got 'em here ; " and he held up the collar box and brown paper bundle !

" Is that all ? " I gasped.

"Oh, no, sir ! I got ten cents the lady give

me. Do you want to see it?" and he began cramming his chubby hand into his side
pocket.

"No, my son, I don't want to see it."

I did n't want to see anything in particular.
His word was good enough. I could n't, really.
My eyelashes somehow had got tangled up in
each other, and my pupils would n't work.
It's queer how a man's eyes act sometimes.

We were now reaching the open country.
The houses were few and farther apart. The
street lamps gave out; so did the telegraph
wires festooned with snow loops Soon a big
building, square, gray, sombre-looking, like a
jail, loomed up on a hill. Then we entered a
gate between flickering lamps, and tugged up
a steep road, and stopped. Cabby sprang down
and rang a bell, which sounded in the white
stillness like a fire-gong. A door opened, and
a flood of light streamed out, showing the kindly
face and figure of an old priest in silhouette,
— the yellow glow forming a golden back-
ground.

"Come, sonny," said cabby, throwing open
the cab door.

The little fellow slid down again from the
seat, caught up the box and bundle, and, looking me full in the face, said, —

257

" It *was* too far to walk."

There were no thanks, no outburst. He was merely a chip in the current. If he had just escaped some sunken rock, it was the way with chips like himself. All boys went to asylums, and had no visible fathers nor invisible mothers nor friends. This talk about boys going swimming, and catching bull-frogs, and robbing birds' nests, and playing ball and "hookey" and marbles, was all moonshine. Boys never did such things, except in story-books. He was a boy himself, and knew. There could n't anything better happen to a boy than being sent to an orphan asylum. Everybody knew that. There was nothing strange about it. That 's what boys were made for.

All this was in his eyes.

When I reached the platform and faced my audience, I was dinnerless, half an hour late, and still in my travelling dress.

I began as follows : —

"Ladies and gentlemen, I ask your forgiveness. I am very sorry to have kept you waiting, but I could not help it. I was occupied in escorting to his suburban home one of your most distinguished citizens."

THE BOY IN THE CLOTH CAP

And I described the boy in the cloth cap, with his box and bundle, and his patient, steady eyes, and plump little legs in the yarn stockings.

I was forgiven.

ONE OF BOB'S TRAMPS

I HAD passed him coming up the dingy corridor that led to Bob's law office, and knew at once that he was one of Bob's tramps.

When he had squeezed himself through the partly open door and had closed it gently, — closed it with a hand held behind his back, like one who had some favor to ask or some confidence game to play, — he proved to be a man about fifty years of age, fat and short, with a round head partly bald, and hair quite gray. His face had not known a razor for days. He was dressed in dark clothes, once good, showing a white shirt, and he wore a collar without a cravat. Down his cheeks were uneven furrows, beginning at his spilling, watery eyes, and losing themselves in the stubble-covered cheeks, — like old rain-courses dried up, — while on his flat nose were perched a pair of silver-rimmed spectacles, over which he looked at us in a dazed, half bewildered, half frightened way. In one hand he held his shapeless slouch hat; the other grasped an old violin wrapped in a grimy red silk handkerchief.

For an instant he stood before the door, bent low with unspoken apologies; then placing his hat on the floor, he fumbled nervously in the breast pocket of his coat, from which he drew a letter, penned in an unknown hand and signed with an unknown name. Bob read it, and passed it to me.

"Please buy this violin," the note ran. "It is a good instrument and the man needs the money. The price is sixty dollars."

"Who gave you this note?" Bob asked. He never turns a beggar from his door if he can help it. This reputation makes him the target for half the tramps in town.

"Te leader of te orchestra at te theatre. He say he not know you, but dat you loafe good violin. I come von time before, but vas nobody here." Then, after a pause, his wavering eye seeking Bob's, "Blease you buy him?"

"Is it yours?" I asked, anxious to get rid of him. The note trick had been played that winter by half the tramps in town.

"Yes, mine vor veefteen year," he answered slowly, in an unemotional way.

"Why do you want to sell it?" said Bob, his interest increasing as he caught the pleading look in the man's eyes.

"I don't vant to sell it — I vant to keep it;

261

but I haf notting,'' his hands opening wide.
'' Ve vas in Phildelphy, ant ten Scranton, ant
ten we get here to Peetsburgh, and all te scen-
ery is by te shereef, and te manager haf notting.
Vor vourteen tays I valk te streets, virst it is te
ofercoat ant vatch, ant yestertay te ledder case
vor veefty cents. If you ton't buy him I must
keep valking till I come by New York.''

''I 've got a good violin,'' said Bob, softening.

'' Ten you don't buy him ?'' and a look as
of a returning pain crossed his hopeless, impassive face. '' Vell, I go vay, ten,'' he said, with
a sigh that seemed to empty his heart.

We both looked on in silence as he slowly
wrapped the silk rag around it, winding the ends
automatically about the bridge and strings, as
he had no doubt done a dozen times before that
day in his hunt for a customer. Suddenly,
as he reached the neck, he stopped, turned the
violin in his hand, and unwound the handkerchief again.

'' Tid you oxamine te neck ? See how it lays
in te hand ! Tid you ever see neck like dat ?
No, you don't see it, never,'' in a positive
tone, looking at us again over the silver rims of
his spectacles.

Bob took the violin in his hand. It was evidently an old one and of peculiar shape. The

swells and curves of the sides and back were delicately rounded and highly finished. The neck, too, to which the man pointed, was smooth and remarkably graceful, like the stem of an old meerschaum pipe, and as richly colored.

Bob handled it critically, scrutinizing every inch of its surface — he adores a Cremona as some souls do a Madonna — then he walked with it to the window.

" Why, this has been mended ! " he exclaimed in surprise and with a trace of anger in his voice. " This is a new neck put on ! "

I knew by the tone that Bob was beginning now to see through the game.

" Ah, you vind dat oud, do you ? Tat *is* a new neck, sure, ant a goot von, put on py Simon Corunden — not Auguste ! — Simon ! It is better as efer."

I looked for the guileless, innocent expression with the regulation smile that distinguishes most vagabonds on an errand like this, but his lifeless face was unlit by any visible emotion.

Drawing the old red handkerchief from his pocket in a tired, hopeless way, he began twisting it about the violin again.

" Play something on it," said Bob. He evidently believed every word of the impromptu

explanation, and was weakening again. Har-
rowing sighs — chronic for years — or trickling
tears shed at the right moment by some grief-
stricken woman never failed to deceive him.

"No, I don't blay. I got no heart inside of
me to blay," with a weary movement of his
hand. He was now tucking the frayed ends of
the handkerchief under the strings.

"*Can* you play? " asked Bob, grown suddenly suspicious, now that the man dare not
prove his story.

" Can I *blay?* " he answered, with a quick
lifting of his eyes, and the semblance of a smile
lighting up his furrowed face. " I blay te Men-
delssohn Concerto in te olt Academy in Vour-
teenth Street ; ant ven Alboni sing, no von in
te virst violins haf te obbligato but me, ant dere
is not a pin drop in te house, ant Madame Alboni send me all te flowers tey gif her. Can I
BLAY ! "

The tone of voice was masterly. He was a
new experience to me, evidently an expert in
this sort of thing. Bob looked down into his
stagnant, inert face, noting the slightly scorn-
ful, hurt expression that lingered about the
mouth. Then his tender heart got the better of
him.

" I cannot afford to pay sixty dollars for another violin," he said, his voice expressing the sincerity of his regret.

"I cannot sell him vor less," replied the man, in a quick, decided way. It would have been an unfledged amateur impostor who could not have gained courage at this last change in Bob's tone. "Ven I get to New York," he continued, with almost a sob, "I must haf some money more as my railroad ticket to get anudder sheap violin. Te peoples will say it is Grossman come home vidout hees violin — he is broke. No, I no can sell him vor less. Tis cost one hundret ant sefenty-vive dollar ven I buy him."

I was about to offer him five dollars, buy the patched swindle, and end the affair (I had pressing business with Bob that morning) when he stopped me.

"Would you take thirty dollars and my old violin ? "

The man looked at him eagerly.

"Vere is your violin ? "

"At my house."

"Is it a goot von ? Stop a minute " — For the third time he removed the old red silk hand-kerchief. "Draw de bow across vonce. I know aboud your violin ven I hears you blay."

Bob tucked the instrument under his chin and drew a full, clear, resonant tone.

265

The watery eyes glistened.

"Yes, I take your violin ant te money," in a decided tone. "You know 'em, ant I tink you loafe 'em too."

The subtle flattery of this last touch was exquisitely done. The man was an artist.

Bob reached for a pad, and with the remark that he was wanted in court or he would go to his house with him, wrote an order, sealed it, and laid three ten-dollar bills on the table.

I felt that nothing now could check Bob. Whatever I might say or do would fail to convince him. "I know how hard a road can be and how sore one's feet can get," he would perhaps say to me, as he had often done before when we blamed him for his generosities.

The man balanced the letter on his hand, reading the inscription in a listless sort of way, picked up the instrument, looked it all over carefully, flecked off some specks of dust from the finger-board, laid the violin on the office table, thrust the soiled rag into his pocket, caught up the money, and without a word of thanks closed the door behind him.

"Bob," I said, the man's absolute ingratitude and my friend's colossal simplicity irritating me beyond control, "why in the name of common sense did you throw your money away on a

266

sharp like that? Did n't you see through the whole game? That note was written by himself. Corunden never saw that fiddle in his life. You can buy a dozen of them for five dollars apiece in any pawnshop in town."

Bob looked at me with that peculiar softening of the eyelids which we know so well. Then he said thoughtfully, " Do you know what it is to be stranded in a strange city with not a cent in your pocket, afraid to look a policeman in the face lest he run you in? hungry, unwashed, not a clean shirt for weeks? I don't care if he is a fraud. He shan't go hungry if I can help it."

There are some episodes in Bob's life to which he seldom refers.

" Then why did n't he play for you? " I asked, still indignant, yet somewhat touched by an intense earnestness unusual in Bob.

" Yes, I wondered at that," he replied in a musing tone, but without a shadow of suspicion in his voice.

"You don't think," I continued, " he 's such a fool as to go to your house for your violin? I 'll bet you he 's made a bee line for a rum mill; then he 'll doctor up another old scraper and try the same game somewhere else. Let me go after him and bring him back."

Bob did not answer. He was tying up a bundle of papers. The violin lay on the green-baize table where the man had put it, the law books pushed aside to give it room. Then he put on his coat and went over to court.

In an hour he was back again — he and I sitting in the small inner office overlooking the dingy courtyard.

We had talked but a few moments when a familiar shuffling step was heard in the corridor. I looked through the crack in the door, touched Bob's arm, and put my finger to my lips. Bob leaned forward and watched with me through the crack.

The outer office door was being slowly opened in the same noiseless way, and the same man was creeping in. He gave an anxious glance about the room. He had Bob's own violin in his hand; I knew it by the case.

"Tey all oud," he muttered in an undertone.

For an instant he wavered, looked hungrily towards his old violin, laid Bob's on a chair near the door, stepped on tiptoe to the green-baize table, picked up the Cremona, looked it all over, smoothing the back with his hands, then, nestling it under his chin, drew the bow gently across the strings, shut his eyes, and began the andante of the Concerto, — the one he had played at the old Academy with Alboni, — not with its full volume of sound or emphasis, but with echoes, pulsations, tremulous murmurings, faint breathings of its marvellous beauty. The instrument seemed part of himself, the neck welded to his fingers, the bow but a piece of his arm, with a heart-throb down its whole length.

When it was ended he rubbed his cheek softly against his old comrade, smoothed it once or twice with his hand, laid it tenderly back in its place on the table among the books, picked up Bob's violin from the chair, and gently closed the door behind him.

I looked at Bob. He was leaning against his desk, his eyes on the floor, his whole soul filled with the pathos of the melody. Suddenly he roused himself, sprang past me into the other room, and, calling to the man, ran out into the corridor.

"I could n't catch him," he said in a dejected tone, coming back all out of breath, and dropping into a chair.

"What did you want to catch him for?" I asked; "he never robbed you."

269

ONE OF BOB'S TRAMPS

" Robbed me ! " cried Bob, the tears starting to his eyes. " Robbed *me!* Good God, man ! Could n't you hear ? I robbed *him!* "

We searched for him all that day — Bob with the violin under his arm, I with an apology.

But he was gone.